DR LURGIE

Jamie Rix

Illustrated by
Sue Heap

Hippo

Other books by Jamie Rix:

Grizzly Tales for Gruesome Kids
Ghostly Tales for Ghastly Kids

Scholastic Children's Books,
Commonwealth House, 1–19 New Oxford Street,
London WC1A 1NU, UK
a division of Scholastic Ltd
London ~ New York ~ Toronto ~ Sydney ~ Auckland

First published by Scholastic Publications Ltd, 1994
This edition published by Scholastic Ltd, 1996

Text copyright © Jamie Rix, 1994
Illustrations copyright © Sue Heap, 1994

ISBN: 0 590 13363 2

Typeset by AJ Latham, Houghton Regis, Bedfordshire
Printed by Cox & Wyman Ltd, Reading, Berkshire

CONTENTS

For my parents
Brian and Elspet

Who always sent me
to school, even when
I protested that I'd got
the Dreaded Lurgie

CHAPTER 1

The Iron Gates

A high ball looped over the dead tree stump and was met by a crashing dive from Frank.

"Goaaaaal!" shouted his team-mates.

"Missed," said the goalkeeper.

"Whoops!" grimaced Frank. "Sorry."

"You complete and utter donkey-brain!" sulked Ben as he took off his goalkeeping gloves. "Now we'll never get it back." The ball had flown off the top of Frank's head over the wooden fence and into next door's back garden, where the old witch lived.

"It was an accident," he protested as his schoolmates turned their backs on him and sloped off to the other side of the playground. "The ball was meant to go in the goal."

1

But nobody was listening.

A little boy with a thick mop of blond curls tugged at Frank's sleeve. "You know that ball which just went over the fence," he said. "Well, I bet you wish it hadn't." He took his thumb out of his mouth. "Now you'll have to go round after school to get it."

"I know that!" snapped Frank, crossly. "I'm not a complete weedy cheeseball, unlike somebody I could mention. . . Like *you*!" Normally, one would not expect to get away with such a rude remark, but Arthur (for that was the name of the boy with thick blond curls) was Frank's younger brother, and younger brothers are completely different. The only reason that younger brothers are born at all, is so that they can soak up the constant flow of verbal humiliation and physical punishment inflicted upon them by their elder brothers.

As Frank came out of school, later that afternoon, his stomach jiggled and sank to just below his knees. It felt as if he had eaten a sack of rocks for lunch, whereas he had, in fact, just eaten fish cakes. His heart pounded like a war drum, his knees trembled like an Olympic springboard, and

his face wouldn't stop twittering. There was no denying that he was scared.

"Why?" enquired Arthur who was holding Frank's clammy hand.

"Wouldn't you be, if you had to knock on that huge front door and ask *that woman* for your ball back?" snapped Frank.

"No," replied Arthur, with an air of feigned indifference. "Not particularly."

"Good. Then you do it," said Frank, steering his younger brother towards the big, black iron gates.

Behind the gates stood a tall grey building. It looked like an old castle. Green ivy tumbled from the cracks between the huge blocks of stone, which had been used to build the walls some six hundred years before. The windows were barred and shuttered to keep out the daylight, and a

crumbling rampart ran around the edge of the raked slate roof which climbed steeply to a central tower. On top of the tower sat a gargoyle. Its hideous face leered at passers-by, and confirmed Frank's deepest fear, that the house was indeed evil.

Frank and Arthur didn't know it, but they were being watched. A video camera, bolted to the gate post, jerked into life and spied on them as they shuffled their feet on the pavement outside the old woman's house.

"Actually," said Arthur, changing his mind, rapidly, "it is your football, and you did kick it over!"

"I did not!" said Frank.

"Liar!" shouted Arthur.

"I *headed* it!" sneered Frank. "There is a difference, you know."

"Well, anyway," said Arthur. "I'm not going. I'm too young to die!"

"Baby!" said Frank, feeling a lot like one himself.

Frank could not really blame Arthur. The house was hardly welcoming. Red droplets dripped like warm blood from a freshly painted sign which hung off the iron railings.

KEEP OUT
IF YOU KNOW
WHAT'S GOOD
FOR YOU

Pinned on to the tangle of barbed wire, which twisted wickedly around the old woman's withered roses, was a smaller notice. Its message, though, was writ just as large.

NO LOOKING OR SMELLING OR ELSE!

But the one that drove fear into the darkest corners of Frank and Arthur's hearts was the inscription carved into the brickwork above the front door:

CHILDREN NOT WELCOME

it declared, in a cold, chiselled, direct sort of a way.

Little wonder that Frank and Arthur stood quaking beneath the big, black iron gates. Little wonder that Frank was seriously considering forgetting all about his stupid football and going home for tea.

"What do you want?" demanded a thin, crackly voice, unexpectedly. It squeaked out of a speaker in the gatepost just above their heads. Frank grabbed Arthur, and Arthur grabbed Frank. They clutched on to each other so tightly that they looked like a pair of Siamese twins. Their arms and legs were frozen together in fear. A raven screeched high up in the grey tower. Then it swooped down and landed awkwardly on the gate in front of them.

"If you don't get lost," said the mean little voice, "I'll have this bird peck your eyes out!" Frank and Arthur took one look at the raven's hooked beak and fled.

"Faster!" shouted Frank to Arthur, who was trailing badly. "The raven's after us!" Arthur was crying.

"I can't," he wailed. "My legs are too short."

"It's catching you up!" screamed Frank. "Take cover!" The raven swooped low over Arthur's head and dug its claws into his soft, blond curls. There was a rip, a tear and a scream, and the raven flew off with a clump of Arthur's hair in its talons.

Arthur's satchel spilled its contents into the road as he fell to the ground. A passing car ran straight over his ruler and snapped it in half. Blue ink squirted ten feet into the air as his fountain pen was flattened to a pulp.

Frank had turned as white as a milk drop. His younger brother lay face down on the pavement, his hands clutching his sore head. Neither moved. Then, suddenly, Arthur stood on his head and sucked his thumb.

"Sorry," said Frank, approaching his upside-down brother apprehensively. "Are you all right?"

"My head is cold," said Arthur. "Why?"

"Because you're a bit bald," replied Frank. Arthur sprang to his feet and put his nose right up against Frank's.

"Right!" he said, firmly. "Let's go home for tea."

The football was forgotten for the moment, and the net curtain, which twitched in the window at the top of the grey castle, went unnoticed.

CHAPTER 2

Old Ma McCracken

Two sunken black eyes peered out from behind the yellow net curtain. Five pearly nails drummed the Death March on the window pane. One set of false teeth lay, motionless, on the back of a greasy old armchair. The old woman picked them up, dusted off the cat's hairs and popped them into her mouth with a slurp.

There was a small rasping noise in the back of her throat as she watched Frank and Arthur disappear into their house next door. Then her mouth pinched up, her lips drew together like the top of a gym bag, and she spat. A long trail of sticky saliva shot between her rice-paper lips and pinged into a bucket by the fireplace. She fingered the

brooch on her moth-eaten old cardigan, stroking the long pin which held it on.

"I *hate* children!" she muttered venomously. A sharp pain shot up her arm. She had stuck the brooch pin right through the top of her finger. The old woman cursed, threw the black cat off her lap and crabbed her way over to her secret stash of gin, which she kept hidden away in a whisky bottle on the sideboard. She took a swig, swilled the gin around her mouth and grimaced as she swallowed it. The old woman hated gin. It tasted like pink medicine to her, but it took away the pain in her finger.

"I really do hate children," she muttered to herself. "I hate their cheerful, smiling faces, their 'aren't we so clever', up-the-sleeve giggling, and their stupid, dumb laughter. Nobody should be that happy! I hate the smell of soap and toothpaste which wafts off them when they go to school in the morning. I hate their scabby knees and their pink bows. And don't talk to me about pigtails! Little blonde pigtails, bouncing up and down on top of their pretty wee heads, like a couple of rats' tails. Show me a world without children and I'll show you one deliriously happy old woman!"

She always talked to herself. She was as daft as a brush.

For someone who reviled children as much as this old woman did, it seemed rather peculiar that she had chosen to live right next door to a school, but then maybe she had an ulterior motive. Maybe she lived next door to a school so that she could watch the children all day, and dream up wicked schemes to destroy them. Maybe. . .

The old woman's name was Angina Lurgie McCracken, Angina to her friends. Not that she had any friends, so nobody ever called her that. They never called her Lurgie, either. She had always hated that name and had kept it a closely guarded secret all her life. Only Frank and Arthur knew about it. Many was the time that they had heard her arguing with herself, through their open bedroom window, and use the name Lurgie against herself, as a final, crushing insult. Armed with this secret knowledge, Frank and Arthur had given her a nickname: The Dreaded Lurgie, but they never used it to her face. They were far too scared of her evil powers to do that!

She was Scottish. She had been brought up on a wild and windy island off the north coast of Scotland, and had lived there, as an only child, with her parents and three thousand sheep. Throughout her childhood she had never had a friend. She had never learned to play like a child, or think like a child, or even feel like a child. She had had more in common with the sheep, and let's face it, sheep are not good company at the best of times.

At the age of eighteen, her father had married her off to Mr McCracken, a hairy, red-faced fisherman, who owned a rowing boat and a licence to fish in the deep waters of Loch McGool. Old Ma McCracken had hated him. It was not that he was a bad man, because he wasn't. He had put food on the table every night. He had never complained about his wife's smelly black clothes, which hung off her shoulders like dishcloths on a washing line.

He had tolerated her cats, of which she kept one hundred and thirty-three, and not once did he object to her foul habit of spitting at him in bed. It must, therefore, have come as quite a shock to him, when, one day, Old Ma McCracken filled his wellington boots and trouser pockets with an assortment of heavy stones and pushed him into the loch. After the funeral she had moved down south and settled in the big house with the gargoyle on top.

Her reputation amongst the children of the town was fearsome. The Scouts had stopped calling at her front door during Bob-A-Job week, because she used to poke

them with an electric cattle prod through the letterbox. When children tried to help her across the road, she would fly into an uncontrollable rage, hit them with her rolled-up umbrella and call a policeman. Sometimes, in the dead of night, she would scuttle down to the kids' playground, and loosen all the nuts and bolts on the apparatus. In the morning, she would sit on a bench, pretending to feed the pigeons, and watch the children crash to the ground as the swings, roundabouts and slides collapsed under their weight. Then she would laugh.

Old Ma McCracken's problem was quite simple. She didn't understand children, so she didn't trust them. In fact, she believed, emphatically, that children had been put on this planet for one reason and one reason only – to make *her* life a misery. Of course, this wasn't true, but you try telling that to a smelly old woman, dressed like a witch, whose heart has the emotional capacity of a caramelized prune.

One day, Frank and Arthur had offered to do her shopping for her. They hadn't wanted to, but their mother had insisted.

"Poor Mrs McCracken," she had said. "She lives next door all by herself. Don't you think it would be nice to extend the hand of friendship?"

"No," Frank and Arthur had replied together. "She eats babies for breakfast, she's got a cauldron in her kitchen for boiling down bones and she takes her teeth out and pinches us with them."

"Stuff and nonsense," their mother had said, "she's just lonely. Now, off you go."

The two boys had gone, reluctantly.

"You want to fetch my shopping for me. Why?"

"To help you out, Mrs McCracken," Frank had said. Arthur was saying nothing. He was hiding behind Frank's anorak.

"You horrible wee stoat! You snivelling wee liar. You deserve to have your eyelids rolled back and skinned with a potato peeler. I know what you're up to. You're trying to poison me! You'll fetch my groceries and you'll sprinkle rat poison all over them."

"No, I won't," Frank had said.

"Aye, you will. You're all the same, you kids. No respect for your elders. Come inside and let me chop your fingers off."

"No thank you," Frank had stammered. "It's awfully kind of you to offer, but we must be getting back."

"And what's wrong with your wee brother?" Old Ma McCracken had said, reaching forward and grabbing Arthur firmly by his nose. "Has the cat got his tongue?" Arthur had shaken his head in a panicky-sort-of-way. "No?" she had cackled, rummaging through her bulky, black skirts. "Well, it has now!"

Old Ma McCracken had then produced the thinnest, hungriest-looking cat that Frank and Arthur had ever seen. She had pinched Arthur's nose until he had opened his mouth to breathe, whereupon the cat had leapt from her arms, and dug its razor-sharp claws into Arthur's tasty-looking tongue. Arthur had screamed. Frank had hit the cat. Old Ma McCracken had hit Frank, and the door had then been slammed firmly in the two boys' faces.

That was Old Ma McCracken, *then*. Not exactly the world's most friendly neighbour.

Old Ma McCracken, *now*, however, was far worse. Not kind, not generous, not even

approachable in the street. In fact, definitely *not* Miss Lovely Granny of the Year.

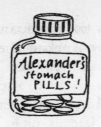

CHAPTER 3

The King's Head

There was a flurry of excitement in Frank and Arthur's household. Mr and Mrs Fleming were charging up and down the stairs, shouting at each other.

"Don't forget my stomach pills!" bellowed Mr Fleming from the sitting room.

"I've told you already, Alexander, they're packed!" came the irritated reply from Mrs Fleming, who was in the bathroom. "Have you got the camera?"

"I'm looking for it now!" replied Mr Fleming, as he rushed into the dining room and slipped on a model fire engine. "Those damned children!" he muttered to himself. "Thank heavens for holidays!"

They were going to Barbados for a three

21

month holiday of a lifetime, which meant that they were not taking the children. Aunt Josephine was coming down from Loughborough to look after them. Frank and Arthur liked Aunt Josephine. She let them stay up late at night and watch the telly, she made the most delicious lemon biscuits ever invented and she could build a kite out of a black plastic bin liner and two bamboo sticks, that could fly all day on a whisper of a breeze.

"If you ask me about your blasted stomach pills one more time, I shall flush them down the loo!" screeched Mrs Fleming, as she crossed the landing with an armful of towels and disappeared into the bedroom.

"There's no need to get angry, Frances," rejoined Mr Fleming, who was struggling up the stairs with a lilo and his scuba-diving gear. "I just don't want to be caught short with a gippy tummy, that's all."

"Oh, do stop being so English!" came the barbed reply. "The food in Barbados is lovely. Why should the hotel chef want to poison you?"

"I don't know," said Mr Fleming,

following his wife into the bedroom, "but you know how much I loathe curry!"

Mrs Fleming screamed with frustration, to which Mr Fleming responded, pathetically, "What? What have I said now?"

"They eat curry in India!" shouted Mrs Fleming. Then, the bedroom door was slammed shut and the arguing stopped.

Frank and Arthur were sensibly staying well out of their parents' way. They were hiding in their bedroom, waiting for the packing to finish and for their parents to turn back into civilized human beings.

It was not, as you might expect, a normal bedroom, because Arthur was not a normal boy. For some reason best known to himself, Arthur liked to spend as much time as possible standing on his head. He would watch television upside down, read a book upside down, (which is incredibly difficult! If you don't believe me, you should try it, now), he would brush his teeth upside down, and sleep upside down, which is why his nickname was Fruit Bat. The only thing that Arthur *had* to do the right way up, was go to the loo.

As a result of this somewhat peculiar

habit of Arthur's, the boys' bedroom was
split in two. Frank's side of the room
contained a bed, a desk, some shelves and a
chest of drawers. Arthur's side of the room
contained much the same sort of furniture,
but it was the way it was arranged which
was so important. Everything on Arthur's
side of the room was upside down. It was
the wrong way up, or, at least, it would be
to you and me. Not to Arthur, though.

His bed was not a bed at all. It was a set
of parallel bars, which was suspended from
the floor by four thick skipping ropes. I say
"suspended from the floor", because the

floor carpet was on the ceiling and the lining paper from the ceiling was pasted to the floor. His pictures and posters were hanging the wrong way round, his toys and books were nailed to the underside of a large stack of shelves, and his desk was stuck to the floor, (which, if you remember, was on the ceiling), with extra strong ThixoFix. The glue proved most effective at securing the desk in its inverted position, but whenever Arthur sat at it and opened a bottle of ink to fill his fountain pen, the ink would run straight out of the bottle and make a huge, soggy, blue stain on the ceiling below.

Confused? I'm not surprised! It would have been simpler for Arthur to have gone and lived in Australia, on the other side of the world, where everything is upside down to begin with. But he couldn't afford it. It takes a long time to save the air fare to Australia when you only get ten pence a week pocket money.

"Why won't the old witch let you have your football back?" said Arthur.

"Probably because she's jealous," replied Frank. "She's not as good at scoring goals as me, so she'll do everything in her power to stop me from practising."

"So that you'll stop getting better?"

"Exactly!" moaned Frank, kicking Arthur's teddy bear. "Meanwhile she becomes as good as Gary Lineker, by practising with *my* football!"

"Do you mean to say," continued Arthur, "that she might end up playing centre forward for the school team?"

"It's possible," admitted Frank.

"But not likely," added Arthur. Frank paused and thought for a moment.

"No," he said, finally. "It's not likely. Can you imagine, sharing a bath with old Ma McCracken after a match? She wouldn't have any clothes on!"

Arthur turned green. His mouth curled up at the edges. "That makes me feel quite sick," he said quietly.

Arthur stuck his thumb in his mouth and Frank had a brilliant idea.

"What would The Dreaded Lurgie least expect me to do?" he asked, suddenly.

Arthur jiggled his feet over his head while he thought. "Fly an aeroplane?" came the response. "Put your head in a lion's mouth?"

"No," said Frank. "Ring on her doorbell and ask for my ball back."

Arthur came down off his head. "You're stark-staring mad and bonkers," he exclaimed. "You can't go into *her* garden. It's not safe. She'll peg you out on the grass, put honey on your eyeballs and set her big, black, eye-pecking raven on you!"

"Do you think she would?" Frank looked worried. "No. She'd never do that!" he added, bravely.

Arthur was quite overcome with nervous excitement. "Well, maybe not, but she wouldn't think twice about boiling up your bones into a huge vat of glue! Or she'd turn you into a television aerial and screw you on to her chimney stack! Or . . . or. . . or. . ." He was quite lost for words. ". . .OR SHE'D JUST KILL YOU!" he blurted out. Arthur was shaking with fear.

Frank sat as still as a Buddhist monk. Then, he smiled. It was a smile of supreme self-confidence. "You're wrong," he said to Arthur. "I know how to get my ball back without her seeing me."

"How?"

"They don't call me 'the cat' for

nothing," boasted Frank.

"They don't call you 'the cat' at all," observed Arthur. "So what are you talking about?"

"I'm going over the wall!"

Arthur felt the blood drain out of his face. "In which case, I am not coming with you!" he said, definitively, kicking his legs back over his head.

Frank's father was slamming cupboard doors in the kitchen as Frank strolled past him and opened the back door. "Is it you who's stolen the insect repellent?" he snapped, crossly.

"No," said Frank. He didn't even know what the insect repellent looked like.

"Then where is it?"

"I don't know," replied Frank.

Mr Fleming threw back his head in despair and hissed at Frank through clenched teeth. "What's the point of having sons, if they don't know where the insect repellent is," he muttered. Then, as he stormed out of the room, he added, "Your Aunt Josephine will be here soon, so don't go out for long."

"I won't," said Frank, wondering why

holidays made his parents so unhappy.

Frank slipped out of the back door and ran along the side of the wall which divided their garden from Old Ma McCracken's. He kept his head down in case she was watching out of a back window. The top of the wall was covered with shards of broken glass and twisted lengths of rusty barbed wire. Old Ma McCracken did not like visitors. Fortunately, Frank knew a spot, at the far end of the wall, where squirrels liked to meet. He had seen them often enough, scratching away at the broken glass in an effort to clear a patch to play on. This, he had decided, would be his point of entry into The Dreaded Lurgie's garden.

Frank shinned up a lilac bush, which was growing in the shelter of the wall, and hopped up on to the squirrels' playground. There was a ten foot drop on the other side, but a cascade of thick, green ivy, which tumbled off the wall like a long, bushy beard, made a perfect ladder for him to climb down. At least, it would have done, had he not, suddenly, heard a crash of pots and pans in Old Ma McCracken's kitchen. Somebody or something was in there.

"Perhaps it's only a clumsy cat on her draining board," thought Frank, logically. "But then again, perhaps it's not." He could have stood on top of the wall and debated this point all morning, but if it *was* only a cat he would be wasting a golden opportunity to retrieve his football. He decided that speed and indiscretion were of the essence and he jumped. The ground looked hard and rocky as he plummeted towards it, so imagine his surprise on landing, when he bounced straight back up again. It was just like being on a trampoline, and a very springy one at that. Frank's head shot up and down behind the potting shed, his arms and legs cartwheeling in a frenetic

31

flurry of frantic scrabbling. He could not regain his footing.

"Who's there?" said a distant Scottish voice, from inside the witch's castle.

Frank stopped bouncing. It had not been a clumsy cat, after all.

He had fallen on to a huge pile of footballs. This was Old Ma McCracken's secret hoard. Every time a ball came over the school fence, she would hide it there. Frank scrambled around for *his* football, but he couldn't find it. There were black balls, red balls, white balls and balls with spots on, but there was no ball with FRANK written all the way round it in blue felt-tip pen.

It was then that he heard the key turn in Old Ma McCracken's back door. The hairs on the top of Frank's arms stood up and

stayed up. His breathing became heavier. His heart thumped like a kettle drum. His mouth drained dry. He had to find his ball, quickly, and then get out of there!

Ducking down between the potting shed and the back wall, Frank edged along the narrow corridor, hoping to find his ball snagged in the undergrowth. It wasn't there. The potting shed, which had hidden him thus far, stopped halfway along the wall. If he was ever going to find his ball, he would have to make a dash across the open lawn and risk being seen. There was nothing else for it! He took a deep breath, hitched up his trousers, and took off.

As he sprinted out from behind the shed, he felt something sharp dig into the sole of his shoe. Before he had a chance to discover what it was, a solid, wooden pole sprang up in front of him and smacked him on the end of his nose. His eyes watered and his nostrils trickled warm blood. What a stupid place to leave a garden rake! What a stupid thing to do, to tread on it! And what a stupid place to stick a football! Frank blinked. "My football!" he gasped, all pain from his throbbing nose now gone. "Look

what she's done to my football!"

Speared on the end of the rake's handle was a deflated, leather football. The word FRANK was just visible in amongst the folds and creases of the shrunken carcass. When King Charles I was beheaded, they stuck his bloody head on a wooden stake and paraded it in public. To Frank, the deflated football looked uncannily like a severed head and he half expected it to bleed. There was nothing he could do now. The ball was useless (about as useless as poor King Charles I's head, in fact). He had to leave it behind and get out of there before The Dreaded Lurgie caught him.

A twig snapped behind him.

Frank froze. A runny nose trumpeted, as it was blown like a fog horn. Frank held the rake in front of him for protection, and slowly, turned round.

A streak of spit shot straight past his left ear.

"So," said the old woman, wiping the dew drop off the end of her nose with the back of her hand. A leather strop hung from her waist. She was using it to sharpen a pair of garden shears. "What have we here?" She slashed the air in front of Frank's nose with the shears, and took one step forward. "An intruder?" Frank thought he might cry. "And such pretty hair!" Old Ma McCracken ran her bony fingers through Frank's shaggy hair. They felt like Twiglets. He was too scared to move. Suddenly, she grabbed him. In a trice, the shears had flashed about his ears and the old woman had claimed her prize. She straightened her back and held a tuft of his hair aloft.

"Now for your neck, you wee trubblemonger!"

As she raised the steel blades above her head, Frank dropped the rake and bolted for the wall. The rake fell forward and clonked the old woman on the top of her head. "Come back here, you wretch!" she caterwauled, shuffling towards him on top of her spindly old legs. "Come back here and taste the cut of my shears!"

But Frank was already halfway up the ivy, and with one bound he vaulted the wall. It was only when he got back inside his parents' house that he noticed the tiny trickle of blood which was oozing from the cut in the top of his head.

"Bit of a close shave at Old Ma McCracken's, was it?" said Arthur, who was hanging upside down off the lightbulb in the middle of the hall.

"Why do you ask?" queried Frank.

"Well, you know when you said that I'd got a bald patch," said Arthur.

"Yes," said Frank. "What of it?"

"Well, from where I am," chortled Arthur, hardly able to restrain his delight, "I can see that you've got one, too."

Frank felt the top of his head and rushed upstairs to find a hat.

Just then, the telephone rang.

CHAPTER 4

A Bolt from the Blue

Mrs Fleming was visibly shaken when she replaced the telephone receiver some five minutes later.

"What is it?" said Arthur, who had slithered down off the lightbulb. His mother was in a daze. She walked straight past him into the sitting room and poured herself a large brandy.

"What's the matter?" said Mr Fleming, who was already in the room, searching the games cupboard for his insect repellent.

"It's Aunt Josephine," faltered Mrs Fleming.

"What about her? Is she not coming? She is coming, isn't she?" Mr Fleming was concerned by his wife's silence. "Frances?

37

Aunt Josephine is coming, isn't she?" he repeated. "We've got a plane to catch in four hours. She can't let us down now. I mean, we've paid for the tickets!"

"No," said Mrs Fleming.

"I have! I paid for them by cheque six weeks ago."

"No. Aunt Josephine is *not* coming."

There was a brief hiatus while Mr Fleming grappled with the impossibility of this scenario. He was shocked and bemused. He gawped at Mrs Fleming, he gawped at Arthur, and he gawped at Frank, who had just walked in wearing a cowboy hat. Then, suddenly, he exploded.

"Oh well, thank you very much, Aunt Josephine! A fine time to call up and change your mind, I must say! Bye-bye, Barbados! I mean, she's only cost us eight-and-a-half thousand pounds, that's all. What's eight-and-a-half thousand pounds to the likes of me? Peanuts, that's what it is! I didn't want to go on holiday, anyway! It was a stupid notion to begin with! I mean, who goes on holidays these days? Certainly not the Flemings!"

Mrs Fleming waited for her husband to stop ranting and then delivered her bombshell. "That was the police on the phone," she said. "Aunt Josephine is dead."

"What?" said Mr Fleming. "Dead?"

"She was struck by lightning as she stood on the platform at the station. Apparently, it was all over in a flash."

"Oh, dear," said Mr Fleming, apologetically. "Oh dear, oh dear!"

"Does that mean you won't be going on holiday, after all?" asked Frank.

"I don't know," replied Mrs Fleming. "The police said that there wasn't much point in us not going, because there can't be a funeral."

"Of course there'll be a funeral," said Mr Fleming.

"Not without a body, Alexander," said his wife, mysteriously. "The lightning fried her to a crisp. It reduced her to a smouldering pile of ashes in two seconds flat. When the fast train from Glasgow flashed through Loughborough station a minute or so later, her ashes were blown up into the air and nobody's seen them since!"

"Oh, good," said Mr Fleming,

heartlessly, "then we can go to Barbados, after all."

"Poor Aunt Josephine," mourned Mrs Fleming. "She never liked travelling by train."

There was now twice as much to be done before Frank and Arthur's parents could catch their plane. The household was put on an emergency footing. A live-in babysitter had to be found, for, despite Mr and Mrs Fleming's callous behaviour over the death of Aunt Josephine, they had, at least, enough good sense to realize that they could not leave two children alone in a house for three whole months.

"I've got it!" declared Mr Fleming to his wife, as she leafed through the Nanny section in the Yellow Pages. "We get the old tent down from the attic, give it a quick dust down, and send the boys off to the park for three months to live under the stars!"

"I beg your pardon?" said Mrs Fleming, incredulously.

"They can live under canvas. There'll be plenty to eat. Bracken stew, a few acorns

and, if the boys are cunning and keep their wits about them, they might be able to catch a sheep or something. Mutton chops for a fortnight."

"Alexander, Frank and Arthur are eight and six, respectively. They are not trained soldiers!"

"No, I know that, but. . ."

"So, the tent is a stupid idea."

"Yes, dear."

"We need to find someone close by, who can live in," declared Mrs Fleming.

"How about the milkman?" offered Frank.

"Ooh, yes!" shouted Arthur. "He's nice, and he could give us rides on his milk float." Frank and Arthur's enthusiasm was dismissed out of court. Mrs Fleming had had a brilliant idea of her own.

"Mrs McCracken!" she proclaimed. "Dear, sweet Mrs McCracken, who lives next door."

"What a thumping good idea!" said Mr Fleming.

"Absolutely NOT!" shouted Frank and Arthur, leaping up from the sofa, as one. Mrs Fleming was slightly taken aback by the vehemence of her sons' reaction.

"Why ever not?" she asked.

"Because Mrs McCracken has just tried to kill me!" said Frank, removing his cowboy hat and thrusting his bald patch into his mother's face.

"Honestly, you boys, just look at you!" laughed Mrs Fleming, patting the two shiny, pink patches on top of Frank and Arthur's heads. "I can't even trust you to look after your own hair. You'll be losing your heads next!"

Frank remembered the mad look in The Dreaded Lurgie's eyes when she had brandished the shears and threatened to slice off his head. He gulped and felt his neck, just to check that it was still there.

Arthur could not understand why his mother did not believe Frank. "Honestly," he said, "she did. She tried to kill him!"

"Nonsense. She's a lovely old lady who wouldn't harm a fly."

"She's a witch," said Arthur.

"Witches do not exist," said his mother. "They are the products of sick little boys' minds."

"She's got a black cat," argued Arthur.

"She's got about a hundred and fifty of them, actually," added Frank. "I wish I had a catapult. They'd make brilliant targets."

"That's enough," said Mrs Fleming. "Come along, Alexander, if we're going to catch our plane, we'd better go and see Mrs McCracken right away."

Much to Mr and Mrs Fleming's surprise, Mrs McCracken was far too busy to look after their two children. She was sorry, and politely declined their kind offer. She did, however, propose an alternative solution. She had an unmarried niece, Nora McCracken, who lived not three streets

away. The old woman did not know her very well, but by all accounts Nora was a pleasant enough girl with a sensible temperament. She was sure that Nora was free for the next few months and would be glad of the extra money. If Mr and Mrs Fleming were agreeable, she would phone her and ask her if she was interested. Mr and Mrs Fleming were not just agreeable, they were desperate. They did not hesitate to declare it a splendid plan, and so it was that Nora McCracken found herself in a taxi, half an hour later, with a hastily packed suitcase at her feet and a huge family Bible on her lap. Nora was an honest, if slightly dull, girl, with a strong sense of moral values and a clear line on cleanliness.

As Mr and Mrs Fleming's Hire Car swept out of the street towards the airport, Frank and Arthur stood on the doorstep and waved. They felt the weight of intense depression on their shoulders. Nora was standing behind them, as erect as a stork. When the car had disappeared, she slammed the front door and clapped her hands, like the infant school teacher she should have been.

"Chop, chop," she chivvied. "Upstairs this instant and tidy your bedroom!"

It was going to be a miserable three months.

CHAPTER 5

The Spice of Life

You might have thought that Old Ma McCracken would have been in Seventh Heaven, having just installed her own personal spy in the Fleming household. Not a bit of it. She was tamping mad. Never before had a small, grubby boy outwitted her in her own back garden! Never before had her silver shears let her down so shamefully. Never before had she been driven to declare, "Never again!"

Cats of all shapes and sizes dived out of her way as she paced up and down her kitchen, ranting at a small damp patch on the wall. She would often imagine that this damp patch was a child. Bizarre, I know, but there it is.

"You imperseverant rancid mome, you!" she bellowed at the top of her voice. "You ninnyhammer! You sloppy, soppy, blockish wee bairn!" She smacked the damp patch with a fly swat, and continued her crazed gibbering. "I hate you all! Away with children, say I. Liquidate the whole puling, giggling, stinking lot of them. I'd like to fry them in oil, set them in jelly, and crunch them down with lashings of whipped cream!"

She picked up a ginger tom, who was too old to move. "It's potion time, Albert!" she whispered to the sleepy cat. "Time to brew." She kissed Albert on his nose and deposited a dribbling circle of spit around his whiskers. The old tom sneezed and returned the favour straight into Old Ma McCracken's eyebrows.

In the cellar underneath her house, Old Ma McCracken kept a cauldron. It was huge and black, and was suspended by four chains above an open fire. Next to it, a gleaming white chest freezer stood out in the gloom. It hummed gently and lent an air of peacefulness to the otherwise dark and forbidding surroundings. Cobwebs trailed

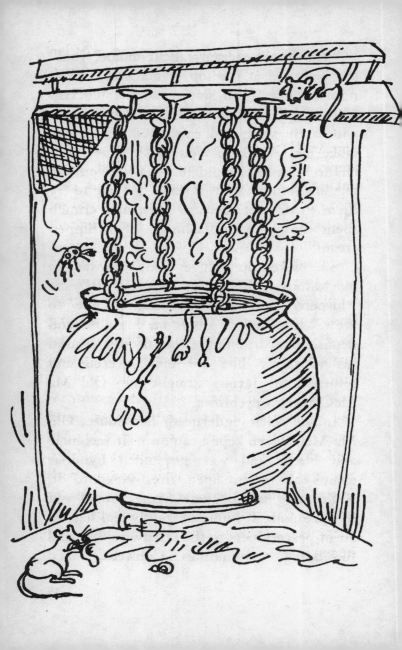

like lumps of knitting from the wooden joists. Rats cavorted in the piles of junk. The smell of decay rose from every corner and hung in the air like a damp cot-blanket.

The cellar door creaked open. A shadow appeared at the top of the wooden cellar steps, followed by a pair of scuffed, black ankle boots. A kitten screeched and shot into the hall as Old Ma McCracken trod on its tail. "Out of my way," she shouted. "There's work to be done!"

The work, as Old Ma McCracken called it, was the mixing of a magic potion. It would be something nasty, of course. Something harmful to children. Something so evil and wicked, that nobody in the history of the world had ever thought of inventing it!

She lit the fire underneath the cauldron, and poured in a barrel of stagnant pond water. A frog leapt out, but Old Ma McCracken caught it and threw it back in. She was a firm believer in cooking with frogs. Without them, a brew was never quite so flavoursome. Then she opened the chest freezer and took out the following items:

A dead cat.
An old pullover.
A jar of wrinkle cream.
Three packets of Bully Beef biscuits.
A glass eye.
The moulted skin of a poisonous snake.
A Senior Citizen's bus pass.
Some furry slippers and a hair net.
A tobacco tin full of stag beetles.
A cuddly toy, (antique, of course).
Some gunpowder.
Her old set of false teeth.
Some bat droppings.
A handful of those folds of skin which
you find under a bloodhound's chin.
A pair of National Health
reading spectacles.
A wooden leg.
Rat poison.
A cupful of powdered whelks.
An old pair of laddered tights.
A bottle of hair dye.
A jeroboam of vintage champagne.
4 battered photograph albums.
Her mother's gold watch.
A haggis.
A death certificate.

A piece of smelly cheese.
The toe-clippings from a goat called
Beelzebub.
Half a dozen good books.
A cracked 78 record of Caruso singing
"The Desert Song."
A spoonful of bicarbonate of soda.
3 tarnished coffin handles.
A shovelful of dirt.
The locks of hair which she
had cleaved from
Frank and Arthur's scalps.
And finally a little dash of salt and
pepper, which she would
eventually add to taste.

All of these things went into her foul concoction.

She put more wood on the fire and stood stirring her brew for five hours. First it bubbled, then it churned and then it shot a jet of scalding steam high into the air. She added more pond water to cool it down and started the whole process again. Occasionally she discovered that a tin or a glass bottle would not dissolve, so she took a hammer and smashed the offending article into a thousand pieces. It still didn't dissolve, but it gave her demonic soup an interestingly gritty texture.

At last the steaming green liquid was ready. It frothed and popped and gave off the most revolting smell. If you can imagine being locked up with an elephant for thirty days and thirty nights, in a room with no windows and no doors – an elephant with an upset tummy, to boot – you're pretty close to imagining what Old Ma McCracken's potion smelled like. The strange thing was, though, that it didn't taste disgusting at all. Far from it. It tasted sweet, and at the same time savoury. It had the sort of taste that would appeal to all tastes. It tasted like

everything you've ever liked, all at the same time.

The other strange thing about this brew was that sometimes it was opaque, and sometimes it was clear, like glass. When it was clear you could see your reflection in it. Only, it wasn't *your* reflection, at all. It was the reflection of you as an old person. All wrinkles and bags and yellow teeth. When Old Ma McCracken took a look at her reflection, all she saw was a skull. She was so old to begin with, that it wasn't possible for her face to get any older.

The old witch was pleased with her work. "Now I'll show those mucky wee brats!" she laughed. She threw her head back, and her sunken eyes sunk deeper and rolled about in the middle of her head.

She rummaged around in the pocket of her dress and produced a fistful of boiled sweets. Then she went over to a shelf at the far end of the cellar, and took down a cardboard box with the word HYPODERMICS printed in big, red letters on the side. From this box she took a syringe and a needle. A long, steel needle, which glinted in the light from the guttering fire. "Come to Granny!" muttered the batty old sorceress, as she unwrapped one of the boiled sweets and sucked up a generous amount of her potion into the syringe. Then, she injected the sweet with the green liquid and wrapped it up again, so that no one could tell that it had been touched. She did this to all of the sweets.

In the sleeve of her dress she kept a crumpled handkerchief. She had never used it because, as you know, when she spat, she spat on the floor. She dipped the handkerchief in her magic potion until it was soaking wet. Then she scrunched it up again and stuffed it back up her sleeve. The green liquid ran down her arm and singed the long black hairs on the back of her hand.

Then she opened her handbag. It was not a normal looking handbag. It wasn't small and neat and shiny. It was huge and bulky, and made from different bits of old carpet, sewn together with cat gut. The clasp was made from the dried head of a dead vampire bat. Inside, the handbag was cluttered with useless bits of paper: telephone bills, Mr McCracken's death certificate, letters from the police asking her to stop shouting abuse at the lollipop lady outside the school. Things that Old Ma McCracken considered unimportant. She tipped the contents out on to the cellar floor, got down on her hands and knees, and sifted through the mountain of junk. At last she found what she was looking for. It was a lipstick. She filled the syringe from the cauldron again and injected the deadly fluid into the centre of the bright red stick. Then, she replaced the lid and popped the lipstick back into her handbag.

Finally, she filled a small glass phial with

her potion, squeezed a cork into the top, and tucked the phial safely into a secret pocket in her bloomers. Then she dusted off her hands, danced a jig and whistled a tuneless little song through her false teeth.

I hate children, and children hate me,
But children love sweeties,
That is plain to see.
They sometimes love their Mummies,
And their Daddies too,
But when it comes to Grannies
They love them through and through!

That night, Old Ma McCracken was a very happy old woman as she slipped between her black nylon sheets. She slept with a smile on her face for the first time in her life.

Arthur Frank

CHAPTER 6

A Wolf in Sheep's Clothing

The next day was a Saturday. Frank and Arthur were always up bright and early on a Saturday. It was their favourite day of the week. On this particular Saturday, however, they were in for a surprise. Through their bedroom window, they could hear Old Ma McCracken singing at the top of her voice. She sounded happy. Frank and Arthur thought this was most unusual, not to say impossible. She was *never* happy. She was always crotchety and bad tempered. It crossed Arthur's mind that something might be wrong.

"She's probably won the Pools," said Frank.

"Not her, she's up to something."

"Perhaps she's just decided to be nice for

a change."

"People aren't like that," said Arthur, wisely. "Nice people are nice all the time. Horrid people are just horrid. They don't change."

As they listened, they heard Old Ma McCracken skip down the stairs, say good morning to her cats and leave the house. They ran to the window and watched her chatting to a rather startled postman by the big, black, iron gates.

"What a perfect morning it is," she said. "Aren't the flowers beautiful!"

"Er . . . yes, I suppose so," replied the postman, who had never heard Old Ma McCracken say anything even vaguely pleasant before.

"Do have a lovely day!" she added. The postman stared at her in total disbelief, and dropped all of his letters. Then she turned on her heel and skipped jauntily down the road, as far as Frank and Arthur's gate.

"She's coming in!" whispered Arthur. "Why's she doing that? She's never done that before!"

Suddenly, The Dreaded Lurgie stopped and glanced up at the two boys in the window. They squeaked and threw themselves flat on the floor.

"There's no doubt about it," said Frank. "She's come to finish the job! She's come to kill us!" They lay absolutely still, held their breath, closed their eyes and waited for the inevitable.

The doorbell rang and Nora answered it. They heard the two women talking in hushed tones. It was impossible to hear exactly what it was they were saying, but from the secrecy in which it was shrouded, Frank and Arthur could deduce that they were plotting. Then, the front door was closed. The two boys bravely stifled their screams. Any minute now, those thick legs in the black, woollen tights would appear at their bedroom door. Any minute now, those silver shears would be flashing about their ears like the giant claws of a flying lobster. Any minute now. . . Any minute now!

They heard the latch click on the front garden gate. They popped their heads above the window sill and saw Old Ma McCracken walking briskly down the road towards the shops.

"Oh," said Frank.

"Ah," said Arthur.

It had not been quite such a close call, after all.

"I've got an idea," said Frank, suddenly.

"Oh, dear," said Arthur. "It's not going to be as silly as yesterday's, is it?"

Frank swung a foot in Arthur's direction and re-shaped his brother's bottom. "No, it is not," he said, crossly. "Anyway, I don't think I'll tell you now, seeing as you're not interested."

Arthur turned topsy-turvy. "OK," he said. "Then, don't."

"Oh," muttered Frank. Then, after the briefest pause, he continued. "Well, the idea is this. You remember I told you that I had seen hundreds of footballs in The Dreaded Lurgie's garden?" Arthur nodded as best he could, considering he was standing on his head. "Well, she's just gone out, right? So, I'm going to go over the wall and steal one. It'll serve her right for puncturing mine in the first place." Arthur seemed singularly unimpressed by Frank's idea, but Frank pressed for a reaction. "Well, is it a good idea or not?"

"I just knew it would be silly," said Arthur in a superior-sort-of-way. "You'll only get caught again, and this time she *will* chop your head off."

"But we saw her go out."

"Frank, she's a witch. An evil witch. She's probably got a broomstick parked round the corner. She could fly back at any second."

"Well, I want to play football," said Frank, decisively, and he disappeared downstairs.

Nora was in the kitchen, singing along with the hymns on the radio. She switched the radio off when Frank came in, and fixed him with a pitying look. "My aunt tells me that you are a naughty boy," she said, bluntly.

"Oh," replied Frank. "Why did she say that?"

"Yesterday, when you climbed over the wall, you trampled on her prize flowers."

"Those weren't flowers," argued Frank. "They were weeds."

"Nasturtiums," corrected Nora. "Just one of Our Lord's many wonderful gifts. She

has asked me to ask you not to climb into her garden again. Do you understand, Frank?"

Frank felt as if he was trapped in a net, and it was Old Ma McCracken and Nora who had a hold on the drawstrings. "Sure," he lied. "Whatever your aunt says! I'm going outside to play in the garden. I'll see you later."

Then, he rushed through the back door, stood in the middle of the lawn and rid himself of the foul stench in his nostrils by filling his lungs with pure, rich, clean, fresh air.

It was easier to climb the garden wall this time. Frank knew where his footholds were, and for some strange reason the wall didn't seem quite so high. A squirrel shot off along the wall as Frank's nose appeared over the top. He squirmed up the last few feet and adopted a crouched position which allowed him to survey The Dreaded Lurgie's garden without being seen from her house. There didn't appear to be anyone about. He took one final look, then leapt down on to the soft mattress of confiscated footballs.

Frank had got it all worked out in his head. He would grab the nearest ball and jump straight back over the wall to safety. No hanging about. No dithering over which ball he would prefer. It was going to be a clean, efficient operation.

Unfortunately, it always seems to be the best laid plans which go wrong. Frank had not reckoned with an uneven bounce when he landed. He had not foreseen the possibility that he might fall awkwardly and cut his knee. But he did. And as he lay on the ground, biting his lip to hold back the tears, he heard the key turn in Old Ma McCracken's back door.

"Oh, dear! Oh dear, oh dear, oh dear, oh dear," said Old Ma McCracken, as she approached the helpless Frank. "Have you hurt yourself, you poor wee bairn?" Frank did not know how to play it. Why was she being nice? And what did she have behind her back? He couldn't see her hands. She was hiding something. It had to be the shears!

The Dreaded Lurgie bent down to take a closer look at his knee and Frank got a terrible shock. The old woman was wearing bright red lipstick. It was smeared over her lips and cheeks like wet paint. It made her look doubly frightening. It made her look like a bloated vampire.

"Shall I kiss it better?" asked Old Ma McCracken, taking Frank's injured knee in her hand.

"I'd rather you didn't, actually," stammered Frank. The thought of those painted lips touching his leg made his flesh crawl.

"Don't be stupid," she persisted. "A little kiss never hurt anyone." And she planted a huge, slobbery, wet kiss on his knee. Her lips were cold and crinkly. It was like being kissed by an ancient codfish.

"I think I'd better be going," Frank said, bravely.

"Nonsense," said Old Ma McCracken. "Your face is grubby. What will Nora say if you turn up with mud all over you?" Her hands twitched behind her back. Frank flinched and edged backwards. If she produced the shears now, he would be powerless to defend himself! "I'll wipe it off," she said, dabbing at his face with the

handkerchief, which had been in her hands all the time.

Frank was very confused. What did she want? What was she doing?

She was offering him a sweet. A boiled sweet. "Go on," she said. "Take it! It'll make you feel better."

"But I've been told never to accept sweets from a stranger."

"Oh, fie on you!" exclaimed Old Ma McCracken. "I'm not a stranger, Frank. Fancy thinking that! I love you like a grandmother, you know that! Come along, I'll take you home and you can suck the sweet on the way."

The Dreaded Lurgie took Frank's hand. She led him through her castle, out on to the street, past the grinning gargoyle, and up his own front path. They stopped by Frank's front door.

Nora was holding a fistful of chicken livers when she opened the door. She took one look at Frank's bloody knee and affected an expression of profound disappointment.

"Now come along, Nora," said Old Ma McCracken, kindly. "Don't be too hard on the wee boy. He meant no harm and he has hurt himself quite badly."

"I'm so sorry, Aunt Angina," said Nora, who was as close to tears as Frank had ever seen an adult. "I did tell him not to climb into your garden."

"Don't fret yourself, girl. Why, only this morning, was I not telling you how much I loved these two boys? How I treasured them more than life itself?"

Arthur's feet appeared from behind Nora's apron. He was standing on his head, at the foot of the stairs, trying to work out what was going on. He was deeply suspicious of The Dreaded Lurgie's new-found concern. Old Ma McCracken lurched forward and planted a huge kiss on his forehead. "Isn't he adorable?" she cooed. "Oh, look, I've put lipstick all over you, Arthur. Come here." Arthur felt safer upside down and would not budge an inch. So, Old Ma McCracken knelt down beside him. She wiped the lipstick off with her handkerchief, and took a boiled sweet out of her pocket. "Would you like a sweetie, too?" she asked, pressing it into Arthur's hand.

"No," said Arthur, throwing it back.

"Of course he would!" interceded Nora, quickly, taking the sweet back again.

"Jolly good," said a radiant Old Ma McCracken. Then she turned on her heels and went back next door.

Nora was very cross. "What have your parents been teaching you?" she scolded. "Have you no manners? When people offer you presents you must learn to accept them. Now, we shall stay here, all night if necessary, until you have eaten your sweet properly!" Then, she unwrapped the boiled sweet and popped it into Arthur's mouth.

Much against his better judgement, Arthur ate it. Magic potion and all.

CHAPTER 7

Things That Go Lump in the Night

The boiled sweets had tasted so delicious that neither Frank nor Arthur wanted to brush their teeth before bed. There was a scene over the sink. Toothpaste flew in all directions. Water was splashed up the red-striped curtains. Mouths were clamped shut and only prised open by the threat of a wallop on the backside. Normally Frank and Arthur liked cleaning their teeth, which only goes to prove what a cunning potion Old Ma McCracken had brewed up.

There were no goodnight kisses that night. Frank turned his back on Nora, pulled the duvet up around his ears, and stared at the wall. Arthur hung upside down from his parallel bars, with his thumb in his

71

mouth, and pretended to fall asleep.

Old Ma McCracken, meanwhile, was sitting in her kitchen watching the clock on the mantelpiece. When it struck midnight, she rubbed her knobbly hands together in anticipation and made a strange gurgling noise in the back of her throat. It was a laugh. A malicious, malevolent rattle, which would have chilled the heart of anyone who had heard it. Fortunately, Frank and Arthur were asleep by midnight, otherwise they might have heard it, and they might have guessed that it was directed at them, and them alone.

Frank started to itch at precisely one minute past midnight. It was his scalp to start with, then the tops of his ears, his nose and finally his whole neck and face. He woke with a start to find his fingers busily scratching away like mechanical diggers. They had raised huge, red welts across his skin, which made him look like the victim of a particularly ferocious lion attack.

Frank leapt out of bed. "Fleas!" he shouted. "Fleas!"

"If you're cold," mumbled a very sleepy Arthur, "get an extra blanket."

"I said fleas, not freeze, you weedy cheeseball! Look at me, I'm covered in horrible, blotchy, red marks. What is it?"

Arthur opened one eye, very slowly. "It's revolting," he said, at last. "I'm glad I haven't got them."

Then, as Arthur watched, a weird transformation took place. Frank's face and neck started to bubble.

"Help!" shouted Frank. "Help me! I'm boiling!"

"I wonder why," said Arthur. He was starting to show an interest in his brother's plight. "It's very odd. I saw a picture of a volcano bubbling like that, once . . . or was it custard? No, it was custard. You know, when you bring it to the boil, and huge bubbles blow up on the surface, and then they burst."

Frank was rolling around on the carpet clutching his poor, throbbing head.

Arthur was caught up with his rather clever custard theory. "You didn't *eat* any custard last night, did you?" he asked.

"No," screamed Frank. "I don't even like custard!"

"Well, I wish you'd told me," said Arthur, "because I could have had yours. I love custard!"

"Will you please shut up about custard and do something about my face!" bellowed Frank.

Arthur dropped off his perch and joined his brother on the floor. "Frank," he said. "It's a bit late to do something about your face now. If you don't like it, you should have sent it back at birth. They won't change it now, after you've been using it for eight years!"

Frank grabbed Arthur by his pyjama cord and tugged him to the ground. "Do something about the BUBBLING on my face!" he wailed.

"I don't have to," said Arthur, in a matter-of-fact sort of way. "It's stopped." And it had. "Only I think you should take a look in the mirror, because something ten times more horrible has taken its place."

Frank hardly dared to look. He covered his eyes with his right hand and stood in front of the mirror. Slowly, he opened his third and fourth fingers and peeked out between them. His jaw unhinged and dropped on to his chest. His eyes pinged out on stalks. His tongue wiggled in his mouth like a sunburnt slug. His face was covered in hundreds of large red boils. He screwed up his eyes in the hope that if he couldn't see them, they might go away, but they didn't. When he dared to look for a second time, the boils stared straight back at him. Big red lumps, like diabolic gobstoppers!

The Dreaded Lurgie, still sitting in her kitchen, was laughing horribly.

Nora was horrified at breakfast the following morning. She flapped around like a mother hen with her tail feathers on fire. She had been left in sole charge of Mr and Mrs Flemings' children and look what had happened to them!

"I told you, you should mind your manners!" she said to Frank, wringing her hands, feverishly. "And now look at you. Unclean of mind and unclean of body!" She fell across the sink in a dramatic gesture of despair.

"You know Thingummy," chipped in Arthur. "You know, him at school, from the family with the runny noses. Well, he got spots all over his face, and, one day, they just disappeared." He was trying to make Frank feel better.

"What made them disappear?" asked Frank, eagerly.

"He bought a balaclava, I think," replied Arthur, "and never took it off."

Frank leapt up off his chair and cuffed Arthur round the ear. His sense of humour had been shot to pieces, along with his complexion. Nora wept to witness such thuggish behaviour. She had never seen its like before and hoped never to see its like again. She pulled the two boys apart and

bustled them out of the kitchen, before they could say another word.

They left for school under a dark cloud. Arthur, feeling wrongly accused for a remark which he had genuinely intended to be helpful. Frank, stoically suffering in silence.

Silence was what greeted Frank as he walked into the school playground. The other children stopped playing and turned around to stare. Frank could have died from embarrassment. One boy, Johnny Pritchard, was meaner than the rest. He came up behind Frank and prodded him with a stick. "Hello, Lumpy," he teased. Then he added, "Bumpy-Lumpy deserves a thumpy!" And he gave Frank a dead leg.

"That hurt!" shouted Frank.

"Well, you shouldn't come into school if you've got the Lurgie, should you?" snarled the bully.

"Frank has not got the Lurgie," chipped in Arthur, supportively.

But Johnny Pritchard had found Frank's weakness. He ran round the playground inviting all the other children to join him in his wickedly cruel chant. "Frank's got the

Lurgie! Frank's got the Lurgie! Frank's got the Lurgie! Ugh! Ugh! Ugh!"

The noise was deafening as the whole school joined in. Frank just stood in the middle of the playground, held Arthur's hand, and sniffed. A huge tear rolled out of the corner of his eye and splashed on to his shoes.

Nora had to come and collect him early from school, because he was so miserable. Matron was nonplussed by his strange eruptions, and the Headteacher suggested that perhaps it would be better if Frank did not return to school until he had seen a doctor. Nora agreed. So, Frank stopped going to school.

Old Ma McCracken's evil scheme was beginning to work.

CHAPTER 8

Doctor-Do-Too-Little

That night, at Nora's request, Old Ma McCracken turned up on Frank and Arthur's doorstep. This time, she did come in. Nora made her a coffee, into which the old lady secretly splashed a few drops of gin, and Nora explained what had happed to Frank's face.

"Oh, dear!" exclaimed her aunt. "How nasty."

"I need to find a doctor," said Nora, helplessly.

"Of course you do," replied Old Ma McCracken, "and only the very best will do. I can give you the name of an excellent doctor on the Balls Pond Road, if you're interested."

"Is he the best?"

"Unquestionably," said Old Ma McCracken. "They used to say that Harley Street doctors were the best, but believe me when I tell you that nowadays, if you want to be treated at the forefront of medical science, the Balls Pond Road is where it's at!"

The following morning, Frank was taken to the Balls Pond Road to see Old Ma McCracken's doctor. His name was Doctor Do-Too-Little. He was a short man with no hair and a pair of half-moon glasses, which perched precariously on the end of his nose. Every time he leaned forwards, he had to tilt his head back and wrinkle up his nose in order to keep them on. He spoke with a foreign accent, and his manner was not what one might call "Grade A-Bedside".

"So you got ze spotz, huh?" This was the first thing he said to Frank, as he walked through the surgery door. "Been eating too much of ze chocolarte, eh? You naughty boy."

"No," replied Frank. "I never eat chocolate."

"Zat so? Ven ve vantz ze naughty boyz to speak to uz, ve vill be askings, OK? Sit!"

Actually, a lot of doctors sound as rude as this to start with, but generally speaking, their bark is always worse than their bite. Not in Doctor Do-Too-Little's case, though. He really was a meany. Moreover, he had a terrible habit of reading the most ludicrous things into a perfectly harmless statement.

"You vant to KILL your MOTHER!?"

"No!" said Frank, startled by this suggestion.

"But you just said quite clearly zat you did!"

"I just said that I don't like chocolate."

"Vich your mother buyz for you?" argued the doctor. Frank was lost. He could not understand what this funny little man was talking about.

"Yes, she does buy me chocolate, sometimes," said Frank, weakly, "but, honestly, it doesn't matter who buys it. I just don't like it."

"You mean, you vant to kill everyvun who buyz you chocolarte?" suggested the doctor, pushing his walnutty nose into Frank's face.

Nora thought that they were getting off

the subject. "Doctor," she interjected, "about Frank's spots."

"Ah, yes, ze spotz. Ze little spotty wotties on his noddle. Vhat about zem?"

"Well, I had rather hoped you might tell us what they were."

"Well, zey are spotz! Any ninkempoop can see zat! Are you blind?"

Frank secretly thought that this doctor was mad, which, of course, he was.

Eventually they were able to get him to concentrate on his patient.

"Az I thought. Zey are spotz," he announced triumphantly after a forty-five minute examination. Frank and Nora knew that! "Zey are big spotz. Come back and see me again in one veek's time. Good day!" And with that the doctor opened the door to his surgery and ushered Frank and Nora out.

You can imagine how disappointed Frank was. He had gone to the doctor expecting a medical explanation for his spots, but the diagnosis had told him nothing that he had not already worked out for himself. Nora was a little surprised, too. If this was the best doctor in the country, as Old Ma McCracken had said he was, then it didn't say much for the rest of them! They had to wait a whole week before they could see Doctor Do-Too-Little again.

And what a week of change that turned out to be.

On Sunday, Frank didn't want to get up. When he looked around his room, none of his toys held any interest for him. They all seemed so terribly young.

On Monday, he didn't like his clothes. His trousers were either too long, too short, too wide or too narrow, and the colour of his shirts far too embarrassing. He would not wear them in public.

On Tuesday, he noticed a small black hair growing underneath his armpit.

On Wednesday, he noticed several more. Not only that, but he was bored. Everything bored him. His comic, his books, his brother, even his video games, which he had loved so passionately only five days before.

On Thursday, his voice took on a life of

its own. He had lost the ability to control it. One minute it would sound all squeaky and shrill and the next it would crack up and sound deep and husky. For an eight-year-old, this was most alarming. But the worst was yet to come.

On Friday, he started to notice girls. Whereas before he had had little time for them, perceiving them only as short, giggly, lumpy things, now he could appreciate them for their beauty, charm, wit and sophistication. He understood why florists did such good business. He only had to see

a girl walking past him in the street and, instantly, he felt this uncontrollable urge to buy her a bunch of flowers.

On Saturday, he went back to see the doctor. He hadn't changed.

"Oh, mein Gott! It's ze spotty boy again. Still no better?"

"Not really," said Frank.

"Damn! I had hoped you might be. Dem spotz is really, UGH! You know vhat I am saying? So, tell me vhat is happening zis veek?"

Frank explained how he had felt over the last seven days, and how his mind and body had been doing things to him which he did not understand.

"He's started shaving," said Nora. "I mean, it's not natural, is it?"

"And he's stopped playing with me," chipped in Arthur, who had come along to see for himself just how batty this doctor really was.

"Do you alvays stand on your head?" said the doctor to Arthur.

"Alvays," replied Arthur, mimicking the doctor's accent. The doctor stared disapprovingly at Arthur, adding to Nora's already massive guilt.

"I haff vun que-vestion," he said quite suddenly. "Did you, Frank, eat anything on ze night before ze spotz appeared? Anythink unushual? Anythink at all?" Frank thought back to the night when he had gone over into Old Ma McCracken's garden to steal one of her footballs.

"I ate a boiled sweet," he said.

"A boiled sveet!" repeated the doctor. "Zen, zere ve haff it! Ze boiled sveet is the cause off zis trouble. Sveeties equal spotties.

You don't need a doctor to tell you zat."

"But I ate one too," said Arthur, "and I haven't got a single spot."

"Zat's because you is stupid," said the doctor. "Any boy who stands on his head must be crackers!"

"But it can't be the boiled sweet," interrupted Nora. "My aunt gave it to him, and she's a dear old lady who wouldn't harm a soul."

"Off course," said the doctor, "ze beautiful Mrs Angina McCracken!" His eyes went all dreamy. "Zen ve must look for some udder reason vhy zis boy is growing older by ze day!"

And that was the truth. He may have been mad, but the doctor had listened to Frank's story, and had worked out what was happening to him.

"Come back in vun more veek, and ve vill see vhat is to be done. Good day!"

During the next week, Frank's development continued apace. He lost his sense of childish fun completely. He stopped watching football, and made strange noises about joining the class struggle and actively supporting the Labour Party. When Nora asked him if he'd like a bedtime story, he said yes, but he'd prefer it if she could read him the cryptic clues from the *Guardian* prize crossword. His taste in food altered too. Gone was his passion for fish fingers, eggybread and Marmite soldiers; instead, he wanted quails' eggs, vinegared winkles and a look at the Wine List. He threw away all of his records by Michael Jackson, Kylie Minogue and Wet Wet Wet, and spent thirty-five pounds buying the latest recording of Wagner's *Ring Cycle* as performed by the Berlin Symphony Orchestra. And he wanted a car. Not a Mini or a Citroen 2CV, but a Porsche. A black Porsche with spoilers and an aerofoil.

Yet, despite all of this, Frank was still the same size as an average eight-year-old. He had an old head on young shoulders. When he went back to see Doctor Do-Too-Little for the third time, he had matured to the grand old age of twenty-four.

For once the doctor smiled when Frank walked in with Nora. He asked them to sit down, while he wandered over to the window and sucked his spectacles. He paused long enough at the window to induce an air of mysterious wonderment in Frank and Nora, before spinning on his tiny heel and leaning over the desk.

Doctor Do-Too-Little was very pleased with himself. "OK," he said. "So zis is vhat I think you got. It startz vith ze spotz all over. Zey *vill* disappear, but as zey go, so you vill start to forget thinks. Your memories vill fade and zey vill be replaced by ze most beautiful daydreamz about deckchairs, comfortable shoes, brass bands, old time dancing at ze Empire Ballroom, and lemonade at threepence ha'penny a bottle – zat sort of think. Your hair vill turn vhite, your eyelids vill droop, and your eyes, your pretty green eyes, zey vill start to cloud over. Your lips vill turn bright blue, your teeth vill vobble and fall out, and then it vill creep into your arms and legs. Zey vill stiffen. Zey vill creak. Zey vill become as if made off rusty metal. You vill get ze horrible tvinges in ze back, your knees vill be sore and your feet vill ache until you haff to sit down and put zem up. Zen it vill be time for ze shrinkink to begin. In truth,

Frank, you vill age. In ze time it takes the earth to travel vunce around ze sun, you vill aged eggs-hactly vun year. Tvelve months every tventy-four hours. In forty days, you vill be sixty-four. In sixty days, you vill be dead from old age."

Frank and Nora said nothing. Frank's face was as white as a sheet. He was trying to come to terms with the doctor's terrible prognosis. Nora was trying to come to terms with how she was going to tell Frank's parents that their eldest son only had two months left to live.

Frank turned to the doctor and stumbled nervously over his words. "Is that really what's going to happen to me?" he asked.

The doctor paused, solemnly, and raised himself up to his full height, which was not very impressive, but it was the best he could do. He reshaped the expression on his face, until it was as honest as he could make it, cleared his throat and prepared Frank for the worst. "Vhy you ask me?" he said, quickly. "I don't know! But it's vhat has happened to me ofer ze years. All I know is zat you is gettink older. Good day!"

Frank put his mobile telephone into his

briefcase, shook the doctor's hand, held the door open for Nora, and left the surgery.

"But he was a fraud. He didn't seem to know the first thing about medicine!" said Nora to Old Ma McCracken, later that night in the Fleming's kitchen. "He offered some wild theory about Frank getting older and when we asked him what could be done about it, he just shrugged his shoulders!"

Old Ma McCracken tutted, loudly. "Fancy!" she muttered. "Who'd have thought it? Appalling behaviour. One thing's for sure, I shall never go back to him again."

"Do you think I should phone Mr and Mrs Fleming," asked Nora, "and tell them to come home?"

"And interrupt their holiday of a lifetime?" exclaimed Old Ma McCracken. "I shouldn't think you'd be too popular if you did."

"But I can't let Frank die."

"Frank die?!" laughed Old Ma McCracken. "You think Frank's going to die! Good Heavens, no. Frank's a healthy eight-year-old. He's got a few spots. Children of his age always get spots. The kindest thing you could do is to stop talking about them in front of him. He must be terribly self-conscious."

"If you say so," complied Nora, meekly.

"I do," said Old Ma McCracken. Then, she got up from the table and went home to make a phone call. It was to thank a certain German strudel-maker on the Balls Pond Road for a little favour he had done her. A German strudel-maker by the name of Do–Too–Little.

CHAPTER 9

The Spider

The Dreaded Lurgie had done her worst. She had spun her web like a venomous Black Widow spider. All she had to do now was bide her time.

As they say, "Everything comes to those who wait!"

CHAPTER 10

Epidemic

But *was* she waiting? Was Old Ma McCracken sitting quietly in her kitchen and bothering no one? If so, why was she going down to the shops and returning with boxes of new clothes? Why had she just paid a visit to the hairdresser for the first time in her life? Why was she spending every night in her cellar? Why had she suddenly taken to returning the footballs which came over her garden fence? And why was she leaving baskets of boiled sweets in the school playground for the children to find first thing in the morning?

These were very interesting questions, but no one sought to ask them of the old woman. Had someone in authority done so, they might have discovered a link between Old Ma McCracken's activities and Frank's disease, which was running through his schoolfriends like a dose of liver salts.

On Saturday mornings, it was quite a common sight to see four or five children following their parents around the local supermarket with brown paper bags over their heads. The newspapers had started to take notice. It was *The Morning Sun* that first drew the public's attention to the plight of the "Boil in the Bag Kids". Others quickly followed, and it was not long before the town was besieged by hordes of ambitious young journalists, eager to snatch an exclusive interview with the frantic parents, or, better still, a photo opportunity with one of the disgustingly spotty children.

The school was closed down. A team of Council workers, wearing white protective suits, arrived with a lorry-load of spray cannisters, full of industrial disinfectant. They sprayed everything. No locker, desk, blackboard or storage cupboard was left untouched. When they had finished, they nailed a sign to the front door, which read:

The Prime Minister was in his office, planning his strategy for the next General Election, when the Minister for Health brought the outbreak of the disease to his attention. The Prime Minister was a bullish man, with a walrus moustache. He hadn't got where he was without courting popular opinion. If the country wished to put its head in the sand and ignore this killer disease, then he could see no reason why he shouldn't do exactly the same.

The Minister for Health, on the other hand, did have a conscience. Unfortunately, there was little he could do about it, voicing his worries, as he did, from such a lowly position within the Government. "What shall we do, Prime Minister?" he asked, nervously.

"We?" replied the Prime Minister, archly.

"Sorry. What shall *I* do?" The Minister corrected himself, and smiled sycophantically.

"Set up a Committee," said the Prime Minister.

"To do what?"

"To appoint a Special Medical Board of Inquiry," came the reply. The Prime Minister had an irritated edge to his voice.

"And what shall they do?" squirmed the Minister for Health. He was wringing his hands with such ferocity that his fingers got knotted together.

"They shall elect an expert to be Chairman, of course," tutted the P.M.

"Whose job will be...?" The Minister of Health was new to his ministerial role, and hadn't yet grasped its finer points. The Prime Minister took off his glasses.

"Whose job will be to do what *all* experts do when appointed to the Chairmanship of a Special Medical Board of Inquiry!" he said, emphatically.

The Minister of Health hardly dared speak. "Which is?" he whispered.

"TO DO ABSOLUTELY NOTHING!" shouted the P.M.

"Oh," said the Minister of Health, popping a little blue pill into his mouth to

bring down his blood pressure. "Good. Yes. Thank you. I think I can manage that." And he bounced out of the room, like the toad that he was.

Everyone was quick to point the finger of blame at Frank. He had, after all, been the first person to catch the disease. But when Nora protested that Frank had not been at school for weeks, and that Arthur had never once shown signs of contracting the nasty red boils, people left Frank alone. And it was true, Arthur was as bright and perky as he had ever been. This was what worried him.

"Why do you think it is," he asked Frank one day, "that I'm the only child from our school who isn't covered in spots?"

Frank was looking at his hairline in the bathroom mirror. "My hair's falling out," he said with alarm. "I'm starting to go bald!"

Arthur sighed. His brother was spending far too much time in front of the mirror these days. "Yes, and you're starting to bulge a bit round the middle, as well," he teased, "but why is it that I'm. . ."

"You don't think I'm getting fat, do you?" queried Frank. He was very worried. He pulled up his striped shirt and tugged at his midriff. "Oh, my God, you're right!" he panicked, kneading great lumps of tummy flesh between his fingers. "This is middle-aged spread. I'm turning into a tubby!"

"Jolly good," said Arthur. "Now, can we talk about me for a moment?"

"Perhaps I should play more squash," said Frank seriously. "I think I should take more exercise. When you get to my age, exercise is important."

"You're only eight years old!" shouted Arthur.

"Going on forty," added a very bitter Frank. "And I still haven't got any kids, or a mortgage, or paid any tax. What am I

doing with my life, Arthur? What is to become of me?"

Arthur looked at his brother from his inverted position on the floor. "I should say that you are going to become a bore," he said pointedly. "In fact, I'll go one further than that. I'd say that you already are one."

"A bore?" said Frank, who was a little hurt by the accusation.

"The world's biggest!" concluded Arthur. "Now, let's talk about ME!" But Frank was not listening. He was checking his gums for Gum-Rot.

Frank would not talk to Arthur, so Arthur talked to himself. "OK," he said. "What?" he replied. "I haven't started yet, you idiot!" he shouted. Then he added, "Sorry!" which was fairly stupid, as he was apologizing to himself. He asked himself a few questions. "Question one: Why have you, Arthur, not contracted the disease? Don't know? Neither do I. Question two: Where does the disease come from? Well, it could come from Outer Space, it could come from an animal, or it could from The Dreaded Lurgie."

Arthur rather fancied the idea that it might have come from Outer Space, but, to his knowledge, Frank had never met a six-headed monster in a space ship. It *could* have come from an animal, but then the doctors would have recognized the symptoms. After all, doctors and vets did exactly the same training. That left only one option. Arthur tapped himself on the shoulder to tell himself that he was ready with his answer.

"It's The Dreaded Lurgie," he said. "She's behind all this, and I'm sure it's got something to do with those delicious, boiled sweets." He posed himself another question, quickly, in order to catch himself out. "How do you know that for certain?" There was a sticky silence. Arthur was angry with himself for asking that question, because he didn't know the answer. So he sulked, and refused to speak to himself until after his bath.

In truth, Arthur *was* sure that The Dreaded Lurgie was behind the spread of this disease. He had a vague feeling of disquiet about something that Johnny Pritchard had said in the school playground.

Something about, "Frank's got the Lurgie!"
It could just be a coincidence that The
Dreaded Lurgie and the disease shared a
common name, but something told Arthur
that it wasn't. What he needed was proof, a
slip of the witch's tongue, a confession from
the horse's mouth itself. He knew it would
be tough to come by, but he would just have
to go on until he got it!

CHAPTER 11

The Public Meeting

That night, Frank slept soundly. In his own words, he was "absolutely shattered". Arthur wriggled, squirmed and twisted, while hanging upside down from his parallel bars. This, however, was perfectly normal, and when he did fall asleep, he slept no less deeply than Frank.

The street outside their bedroom window was quiet. Only occasionally was the stillness broken by distant Scottish cackling, which drifted up from The Dreaded Lurgie's cellar and frightened the moths playing Catch-Tag around the streetlamp. A shooting star, on its way to an old Indian hunting ground in Colorado, heard her

laugh and fell out of the sky.

There were few cars on the road. The odd taxi, a couple of milk floats, and the local doctor's car, a vintage, leather-seated Humber, which chugged its way laboriously from one sick household to the next. The poor doctor had not slept for weeks. As Frank's disease had spread, so the demand for the doctor to go out and treat spotty children in the middle of the night had increased. The doctor was not a grumpy man, but he was tired. As yet another anxious parent called him out at three o'clock in the morning, he secretly wished that he had listened to his own father's advice all those years ago. "Don't become a doctor," his father had said. "Take up golf instead."

Right then, that doctor would have given anything to swap his stethoscope for a six iron.

There was also a blue van, belonging to the local council, which was bunny hopping from one street corner to the next. It was being driven by a ratty-looking man in glasses. Next to him was his wife. She was a strong, powerful woman, built like a pillar box. She had the most extraordinary hair. It was bright blue, where the rinse had gone wrong, and it sat on the top of her head like a crash helmet. Each time the van stopped she fell out of the passenger door clutching on to a pot of glue, a brush and a rolled up poster. Once back on her feet, she looked furtively up and down the road, before unrolling the poster, covering it with glue, and sticking it up on the nearest wall or shop window. In the morning, the whole town was covered with her message. The poster read:

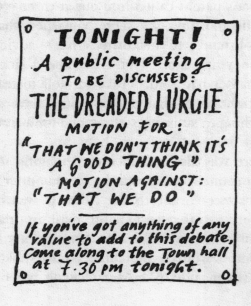

Frank and Arthur saw one of these posters when they woke up in the morning. The woman with the bright blue rinse had, rather pointedly, stuck one up on the outside of their bedroom window. Arthur was immediately struck by the name which the woman had used to describe the disease – "The Dreaded Lurgie". This could no longer be coincidence. The disease *had* to be linked to Old Ma McCracken. This poster was a clue and it gave Arthur an ingenious idea, which he would have shared with Frank, had Frank not been completely absorbed in a grey hair, which he had just discovered on his temple.

The town hall was buzzing, as the hands of the municipal clock shuddered round to 7.30. Everyone was there. The mayor, the lady with the blue hair and her ratty husband, the police chief, the local doctor (who was dozing quietly in a corner), the parents of all the children who had contracted the disease, the parish priest, the local undertaker (who had come along to see just how much his business was likely to pick up), Old Ma McCracken, Nora (who was there to offer her aunt support), a couple of damp dogs and Miss Blackpool, who felt very out of place in her bikini and left soon after the meeting had started when she realized that she was in the wrong room.

Frank and Arthur were at home with a Swedish babysitter. She was a splendid, red-faced girl called Olga. Arthur had requested her specifically, because he had met her once before at a friend's house and, as a consequence, he knew her weak spots. She had a passion for outdoor sports, train-spotting and ice-cream. Unfortunately she couldn't speak a work of English, but this suited Arthur's plan right down to the ground.

"Olga," said Arthur, peeping round the sitting room door. He was in his pyjamas.

"Ya," said Olga. She turned down the volume on the television set.

"Olga," repeated Arthur, creeping into the room with his arms clasped tightly across his stomach. "Frank and I have got bellyache." Olga smiled and nodded. She had not understood a word.

"Mummy and Daddy always give us ice-cream when we've got bellyache, don't they, Frank?"

Frank was still hovering outside the door. He didn't know what Arthur was playing at, but whatever it was, it was stupid and childish.

"Ice-cream, ya!" beamed Olga. She rubbed her own tummy as if to say, I love ice-cream.

"Would you go and get us some?" continued Arthur. "We'd love you for always if you did."

"Ya, ya!" said the babysitter, but she didn't move.

"It's in the cellar," said Arthur. "You have to go into the cellar to get it from the freezer."

"Ice-cream?" asked Olga.

"Yes. In the cellar." Arthur was starting to lose his patience. Then he had an idea. "Follow me," he said, gesturing madly. Suddenly, it all clicked in Olga's head. She pointed at the floor and leapt up from her seat. The springs heaved a sigh of relief. She was a big girl. Arthur took her by the hand and led her to the top of the cellar steps. He indicated that she should go down them.

"Ice-cream, down there!" he shouted slowly, opening his mouth extra wide to accentuate the words.

"Ya!" screamed a delighted Olga. "Ice-cream!"

Then, with only the slightest shove from Arthur, she was propelled down the steps into the cellar, where she crawled around in the coal dust until she found the freezer. She was so excited about finding some ice-cream, that she didn't hear Arthur locking the cellar door behind her, nor did she hear the two brothers leaving the house, and heading off in the direction of the town hall.

"But that," said the lady with the blue hair, "is not really what I came here to speak about tonight." There was an uncomfortable shuffling in the audience. She had been speaking for over half an hour already, and she was boring everyone to death. The mayor stifled a yawn as she continued. "This foul disease, this plague of boils, this Dreaded Lurgie has been thrust upon us for a reason. Is it not clear to all of you here tonight, that God has looked down from His mighty throne in the clouds, He has seen our children and He has said 'No more!' No more childish impudence, no more delinquent behaviour, no more infantile wickedness! He has judged our children and found them to be rude, and cheeky, and thoroughly unpleasant. That is why he has sent this Dreaded Lurgie amongst us. To cleanse the world of its wicked children!"

It was about this time that the door at the back of the hall edged open, and Frank and Arthur slipped in, unnoticed.

"And so, I say to you, this." The blue-haired lady's voice was booming like a fog horn now. "Sack the Archbishop of Canterbury! Sack the Prime Minister! Sack the Queen! I will do their jobs. I alone know what is best for this country!"

That was it. She had finished speaking, and she sat down. There was a stunned silence in the hall. Then, one pair of hands started clapping. One solitary pair of pathetic hands, belonging to the second most pathetic person in that hall next to the lady with the blue rinse. It was her ratty husband, who had just woken up.

Then, suddenly, quite to everyone's surprise, Old Ma McCracken stood up in the middle of the hall, and shouted, "Balderdash!" This was greeted with rapturous applause, and shouts of "Hear, hear" and "Bravo!" Old Ma McCracken bustled her way on to the stage and prepared to speak.

"What is she wearing?" whispered Arthur to Frank. "She looks like a painted doll."

Arthur was right. Old Ma McCracken had discarded her black clothes in favour of a bright dress with green and yellow flowers on it. In her hair she had a huge pink bow, and her face was caked with orange make-up and thick red lipstick. She looked frightful.

She started to speak. "Children are a blessing," she quivered, with an unnatural edge of sentimentality in her voice. "There is no one in this hall who would wish to harm a child." She paused to let the applause subside. "They are the sunshine in our dull lives, they are like wee petals on a rose, to be nurtured and cared for, they are, ladies and gentlemen, our whole reason for living!" She allowed a tear to roll down her cheek, which brought the audience

to their feet. Modestly, she accepted their adulation.

Arthur listened intently, unable to believe what he was hearing. Did these people not know that this sweet old lady, with crocodile tears in her eyes, was none other than The Dreaded Lurgie herself.

"There is no such thing as the Dreaded Lurgie," continued the virtuous old woman. "Sent by God, indeed! It's just a wee infection and, as such, should have a more appropriate name, like Snoggle Spots. It will go away, if we just leave it alone!"

That was it! Arthur suddenly saw the light. Here was his proof. The horse had opened its mouth and spoken. Her denial condemned her. "There is no such thing as the Dreaded Lurgie. . ." she had said. Well, she would say that, wouldn't she? Angina Lurgie McCracken would say that a disease which carried her secret middle name did not exist. She didn't want anyone to make the connection. It would only take one reasonably smart person to realize that the disease was named after her, and her goose would be cooked! And, "It will go away, if we just leave it alone!" – What rubbish! If they followed Old Ma McCracken's advice, Frank and all the other children would be dead within a month. She was misleading the audience. She was deliberately pulling the wool over their eyes!

Arthur snapped! "Stop!" he shouted, leaping on to the stage, and dragging a sheepish-looking Frank with him. The sudden appearance of two small boys, dressed in their pyjamas, caused a stir in the audience. Nora thought that they were at

home in bed and nearly had a heart attack. Old Ma McCracken's lips curled as she recognized them.

"She's a liar! She poisoned my brother Frank with a boiled sweet and now he's dying. Look at him! He's eight years old, but he looks and thinks he's fifty. His hair has fallen out, his teeth have gone yellow, and he's getting his first pair of reading glasses next week! I mean *really* look at him! His skin sags, he can't get up in the morning because his bones ache and he's not interested in football any more! And it's all her fault. She's a witch. She steals children's toys and spits in their faces! Stop listening to her. I'm telling you the truth!"

But the mayor didn't think so, the chief of police didn't think so, and none of the parents thought so. Nor did anyone else in the hall. They thought that Arthur had caught the Snoggle Spots himself, and with it a nasty case of madness. He and Frank were bundled off the platform by a large policeman, to a chorus of boos and catcalls, and deposited in the back of a Black Maria.

As they disappeared, feet first, through the door, Arthur heard Old Ma McCracken trying to calm the audience. "Poor boy," she said. "Such a sweet child. You must find it in your hearts to forgive him. I love him as if he were one of my own!"

The audience were so moved by her generosity of spirit that they burst into floods of tears.

Then she added, "I hope you'll all support me tomorrow, in my quest to become the United Kingdom's Most Glamorous Granny."

And they cheered and stamped their feet and pledged blind allegiance to Old Ma

McCracken until she thought that her evil heart would burst.

The Prime Minister heard about Old Ma McCracken's rousing speech on the Nine O'Clock News. He put down his whisky and soda and picked up the phone. "You see," he said to the Minister for Health. "I was right. Doing nothing is always the best course of action. The Dreaded Lurgie does not exist. What we've got is a mild outbreak of Snoggle Spots. It's not a plague, it's just a 'wee infection'."

The Minister tried to explain why he thought differently, but the Prime Minister had the louder voice.

"So," he shouted, adding extra emphasis to each word to achieve maximum effect, "there is nothing to worry about. Panic over!"

"Yes, Prime Minister," said the Minister, meekly. Then he replaced his receiver and lit a cigarette to calm his shattered nerves. For a Minister for Health he had some very unhealthy habits indeed.

By the time Frank and Arthur arrived home, they had forgotten all about the babysitter. They were too busy defending their rude behaviour to a tragically upset and severely disappointed Nora. She was lecturing them on the need to respect their elders and the ill effects of running through the streets at night in thin, cotton pyjamas, when she heard the snoring. She found Olga asleep on the cellar steps, surrounded by empty ice-cream cartons and puddles of melted "Choc 'n' Nut". This was the final nail in Frank and Arthur's coffin. They were banished to their room, cold, hungry and badly misunderstood.

CHAPTER 12

Operation Sycamore

Arthur switched on his bedside lamp and squinted at his alarm clock. It was three-thirty in the morning.

"Frank!" he hissed. "Frank! Wake up!" His brother did not stir. Arthur flipped down on to the floor and stuck his toes under Frank's nose. He had been so busy during the last week that he hadn't had time to take a bath. The extra strong, cheesy whiff did the trick.

"What. . . Who is it? Where am I? Oh, it's you, Arthur. What do you want?" Frank looked at the clock. "Have you seen the time?"

"It's time for action," declared Arthur, who had been watching too many James

Bond movies. "Let's talk tactics."

"Let's go back to sleep," sighed Frank. "I need my twelve hours."

"In twelve hours, Frank, you will have aged six months. There'll be time enough to sleep when we've defeated The Dreaded Lurgie."

"Don't be stupid," said Frank. "We can't defeat her. She's a local hero. Everyone loves her. They won't believe us!"

"No," said Arthur, "but they might believe *all* of us."

"Who's all?" asked Frank.

"All the children who've got the Snoggle Spots."

"But there are thousands of them!"

"Oh, all right then. Not all, just one or two. I've got this theory. I bet they all met Old Ma McCracken just before they caught the disease. All we've got to do is find them and ask them. What do you think?"

Frank thought sleep. His snoring rattled the windows and shook the foundations of an old folk's home in Billericay.

It was obvious to Arthur that he was going

to have to do this alone. He pulled on his clothes over his pyjamas, and tiptoed to the bedroom door. The handle turned, but the door wouldn't budge. It was stuck. He tugged harder, but it made no difference. Nora had locked the door. She had moved across into the enemy camp, and had nipped Arthur's plan in the bud. He couldn't even get out of his own bedroom.

Unless he tried the window, of course.

The trouble with the window was that it was on the second floor, and there was a twenty foot drop to the pavement. Admittedly there was a ten foot sycamore tree growing underneath the window, but it was virtually impossible to reach, unless you were an acrobat or a monkey. Or Arthur, Super Upside-Down Boy! The only boy who could walk faster on his hands than he could on his feet. The only boy with highly developed, prehensile toes, which looked like a bunch of pink bananas. The only boy in the world who could defy gravity!

Arthur thought it was worth a try.

He slid the bottom half of the sash window up as far as it would go. Then, he sat on the window ledge and hooked his feet around the sides of the window frame. He shuffled his bottom towards the corner of the ledge, closed his eyes and let go. He fell backwards, until he was hanging upside down by his feet. Unfortunately, the tree was still some distance away and Arthur was not quite sure how long he could maintain this uncomfortable position before his back snapped. So, he started to swing. Slowly he gathered momentum – left, right, left, right, left, right, left. . . He let go with his feet and flew through the air towards the tree. He had calculated that with a half twist backward somersault he should just be able to reach the top branch. In fact he did a double twist reverse pike, but the result was the same. He *missed* the top branch. He hit the trunk with a sickening thud and bent his nose. Fortunately, as he slid towards the ground, a lower branch caught him by the seat of his trousers and held him fast. All Arthur had to do now was to drop the remaining eight feet to the pavement. This was easy. He did it by tearing a huge, gaping hole in his trousers. Arthur would have to think up a convincing excuse to tell Nora in the morning. A life or death struggle with a trouser-hungry

Rottweiler seemed the most likely option.

The first house he arrived at was Sally's. It was dark. Not surprising really, it was four o'clock in the morning and everyone was asleep. Arthur took a handful of gravel from the road and threw it at her bedroom window. It rattled the glass and made enough noise to waken the dead. Arthur hid behind a tree and held his breath in case Sally's parents had heard.

After a moment, the window opened and a spotty face peered out. "Yeth?" it said, with a slight lisp.

"It's me," whispered Arthur.

"Me, who?" enquired Sally.

"Me, Arthur!" shouted Arthur.

"Keep your voice down!" snapped Sally. "People might think you're my boyfriend!"

Arthur had never understood the way soppy girls thought, and this remark did little to clarify matters. It was best to get to the point. "How did you catch the Snoggle Spots?" he asked.

"The what?" she giggled. Arthur had forgotten that she had not been at the meeting.

"The Lurgie," he said.

"I don't know," said Sally. "Off your brother, probably."

"No, you didn't," replied Arthur, firmly. "Did you meet Old Ma McCracken just before you came up in spots?"

"Ith she that ugly woman with bad teeth and black thtockingth?"

"The witch, yes."

"She gave me a thweet," said Sally. "I fell off my bike outthide thchool. She picked me up, kithed it better and gave me a boiled thweet. Cor! Doethn't her breath thtink! That thweet was deliciouth. It tathted of pitthaa!"

Arthur allowed himself a smile. "Go back to bed," he said. "I've got to go!"

"Ith that all?" said Sally. "That wathn't very difficult." Then she added, "Would you *like* to be my boyfriend, 'coth you can if you want."

Arthur was out of there.

Next on his list was Johnny Pritchard, the school bully. Arthur didn't like him at all, nonetheless he couldn't help but feel sorry for the nervous, grey-haired man who appeared at Johnny's window.

"She gave me a sweet," he admitted,

"and wiped my mouth with her handkerchief. She said I could have another one if I beat up all the children in the playground."

"Is that why you pick fights with everyone, because Old Ma McCracken tells you to?"

"She scares me half to death," said Johnny Pritchard.

"You won't die," said Arthur. "And don't worry, we'll get her."

Arthur visited another seven victims before dawn. Each of their stories confirmed what he had suspected. The day before their thumping great boils had appeared, they had all met Old Ma McCracken. They had all been kissed, or wiped with her handkerchief, and each of them had been given the most scrumptious boiled sweet they had ever tasted.

Arthur was just hand-springing back through his bedroom window as the sun came up. Frank was still asleep, so Arthur woke him up.

"I've got her!" he said, excitedly. "I know how she does it. She puts poison in the sweets, on her handkerchief, and on her lipstick."

"Perhaps we should tell the police," said Frank, rubbing the bags under his eyes and sucking the taste of decay out of his mouth.

"That's brilliant," enthused Arthur. "I'd never have thought of that!"

"You will when you're fifty-five," said Frank, bitterly. Then he stepped over Arthur's head and went into the bathroom to trim the hairs in his nostrils.

Frank and Arthur went to the police station after lunch, but the police did not believe them.

"Mrs Angina McCracken?" laughed the bearded desk sergeant, whose name was Bill. "'Ere, Ben, come 'ere and cop a load of this!" The sergeant's belly shook as he tried to control his mirth.

Ben was equally amused. "You're trying to tell us that Mrs McCracken is killing off all the children in this town by poisoning them."

"She makes them grow old before their time," said Arthur, solemnly.

"I'm only eight really," added Frank.

This caused a renewed bout of hysterics.

"And I'm the Milky Bar Kid!" screamed Bill. He addressed himself to Frank. "Come along now, sir, let's be having no more of this nonsense. Take your son home and give him his tea."

"You're not listening," said Frank. "I'm not this boy's father, I'm his brother. There're only two years between us." The two policemen had stopped laughing now.

"All right," said the sergeant, "this has

gone far enough. If you two practical jokers don't leave my police station this second, I'll have you both arrested!"

Frank and Arthur looked at each other. What could they do? Arthur thought he could do more.

"So you're not going to arrest Mrs McCracken, then?" he persisted.

The desk sergeant grabbed Arthur by his jacket and pulled him up on to the counter. His bristly beard scratched against Arthur's milky-smooth face. "Mrs McCracken," he said, "is a respected member of the community, and for your information she has just won the local heat of this year's Glamorous Granny competition."

"She's famous!" chipped in Ben. "She is representing this town in the finals, which will take place next week in Birmingham!"

It was Bill's turn to speak now. These two were like a comedy double act, thought Frank.

"So how do you think it would look if Ben and I were to go out and arrest the single most important person in this town, for no other reason than a couple of troublemakers wanted to conduct a witch hunt?!"

Arthur shrugged. Frank wished he was in a wine bar somewhere, where he might lose himself in an ice-cold bottle of Australian Chardonnay.

"Now scram!" bellowed Bill, dropping Arthur to the floor like a lead truncheon.

"Did you notice how young policemen look these days?" observed Frank, when the two boys got outside.

"No," said Arthur, vacantly. He was thinking about something completely different. "Fancy Old Ma McCracken winning through to the finals of a Glamorous Granny competition," he remarked.

"I think the judges must have been blind," said Frank. "It beats me why she entered in the first place."

"Me, too," said Arthur. "I just wish I had the answer. In the meantime, I suggest we start looking for a cure."

"For what?" asked Frank.

"For your old age," explained Arthur. "You haven't got much longer to live!"

CHAPTER 13

Turning Back the Clocks

Let us pause for a moment to consider Frank. Since he had first been to see Doctor Do-Too-Little, he had aged fifty-four years in as many days. He had been transformed from a happy-go-lucky, fresh-faced child into an obsessive, crinkly-faced sixty-two-year-old man. Most of his hair had fallen out and what was left was white. His eyesight was failing, which meant that he had to wear six different types of spectacles. He had spectacles for reading, spectacles for watching television, spectacles for walking down to the shops, spectacles for looking up at the sky, spectacles for brushing his teeth and, most importantly, spectacles for finding all of his other pairs of spectacles. His hearing came and went. On a good day he could hear a pin drop, but on a bad day he would only notice the pin when he trod on it. His lovely pink skin had turned grey and had drooped. The double pleats and folds in his jowls made him look like a particularly ancient turkey. The backs of his hands looked like crumpled pieces of paper, and the skin on his knees flapped about with such ferocity that he got whiplash whenever he walked down the street. His bones had started to ache, especially in the cold weather, and his joints were rusting faster than an old jalopy. And, of course, he had started to shrink. Slowly, almost imperceptibly to begin with, but, sure enough, with each passing day, Old Father Time snatched back one whole centimetre from Frank. One whole centimetre, which Old Father Time would never return.

But what of Frank's mind? That was crumbling too. His memory, once so sharp and retentive, was now only marginally more useful than a lump of burnt marshmallow on the end of a toasting fork. He was knowledgeable, worldly wise and full of funny stories, all of which he had picked up during the sixty-two years of his life, but he just couldn't remember the simplest things. Where he had put his book, for example, or how many eggs in a dozen, or whether black clouds overhead meant rain or sunshine. Bizarre things that you and I don't even have to think about. Recently he had been thrown out of the butcher's when he had asked for a copy of the *Beano*, three chocolate bars and a pencil.

It was this deterioration in Frank's condition which spurred Arthur on to find a cure.

"It'll never work!" protested Frank, as Arthur tied him firmly to the slack tennis net in the local park. "Bones are not designed to stretch."

"I haven't finished yet," said Arthur, grabbing a fistful of helium balloons. He tied two balloons to Frank's ears, one around each of his knees, and stuck a fifth to Frank's bellybutton with Sellotape.

"Now, all I have to do," said Arthur, "is to wind up the tennis net, until it's really tight, and your body should stretch to fit your wrinkles."

"I don't know," moaned Frank. "These balloons make me look completely stupid, not to mention the fact that they hurt."

"They are designed to give you extra lift," explained Arthur, grasping hold of the winder and giving it one good turn to the right. The ropes tightened around Frank's wrists and ankles, as the tennis net was reeled in.

"Ow!" shouted Frank.

"Oh, do stop complaining!" said Arthur. "I've hardly started yet." He tightened the net another two notches and wandered over to see how Frank was getting on.

His face was turning a nasty shade of purple. "You're pulling my legs off!" he bellowed.

"Nonsense," replied Arthur, prodding Frank's thighs. "There's still plenty of give in these. Another three notches should do it!"

Another three notches did do it. They caused Frank to scream so loudly that the park keeper appeared to see what all the row was about.

"What are you doing to my tennis net?" he shouted.

"Using it as a rack to stretch my brother," explained Arthur.

"I'll give you a long stretch!" threatened the park keeper. "Now go on! Hop it! Get out if it!" Arthur untied Frank as fast as he could under the circumstances. The park keeper was twisting his ear into an extremely unnatural shape.

Unfortunately, Frank's wrinkles had not disappeared, as Arthur had hoped. He still looked like a baggy old elephant.

The next treatment was very scientific. It involved psycho-suggestion, which basically meant that Arthur was going to fool Frank's mind into believing that it was young again. They were in the bedroom. He made Frank take off all his clothes and wrap a white towel around his middle so that it looked and felt as if he was wearing a nappy. Then, Frank lay on the bed. Arthur stuck a dummy into Frank's mouth, put a baby's bonnet on his head, a rattle in his hand, switched off the lights and sang him a lullaby.

An hour later, Arthur switched the lights back on. Frank was fast asleep, with a

gooey–sort–of–smile on his face, but he was not any younger.

There was only one thing for it. Arthur had not wanted to resort to chemical warfare, but the Lurgie was proving to be such a powerful adversary, that he had little choice. An antidote to the disease would have to be concocted.

Arthur found an old bucket in the garden, which his father used as a manure carrier. Apart from a few brown, crusty bits around the edge, the bucket looked fairly clean, but Arthur gave it a quick rinse with cold water, just to be on the safe side. After all, he didn't want to poison his brother for a second time. Then he set about mixing his ingredients.

Arthur's first concern was to find something that would rekindle the fire of life which was so sadly missing from Frank, the old man. A bottle of pepper sauce seemed pretty fiery. Plus six chillies, a clove of garlic, two dozen firelighters, some curry powder and a generous slug of something called Aqua Vitae, which he found in a drawer marked "Private and Confidential", in his father's desk.

Next, he needed to correct the thousands of lines and wrinkles which dogged Frank's face and body. Clothes pegs were always useful for pinching skin together – fifteen of those. Some of his mother's make-up; blusher, eye-brow pencil, powder-puff and moisturizing cream. All were mashed up together and chucked into the bucket. Arthur also found a bottle of perfume on his mother's dressing table, called "Young at Heart". It seemed foolish to ignore it, so in it went too.

Finally, Arthur needed to stop the ageing process. He had heard that Japanese people lived longer than anyone else in the world, because they ate raw fish. This was the answer. The trouble was, that there was only one source of raw fish in Arthur's house. He stared long and hard at his two goldfish, Batman and Robin, but decided, in the end, that they were too small to be of any use to Frank. Instead, he opened a tin of pilchards and an economy pack of fish fingers, and threw them in. In the dustbin he found the skeletons of two trout. Their white eyes stared blankly at him like four smokey buttons. He took a teaspoon, whipped the eyes out and flicked them into the bucket, where they floated on the surface and watched his every move, suspiciously.

"Stop it!" shouted Arthur at the eyes. They were making him nervous. The eyes blinked and dived down into the depths of his greasy brew.

Arthur stirred his concoction vigorously. Then, he took a sip. Ever such a tiny sip, because as he brought the wooden spoon up to his mouth, his nostrils detected a yucky pong of puke-making proportions. Frank would never drink this mixture unless Arthur made it taste better. He added some aromatic herbs, a couple of scented tea bags, a slab of chicken fat which had been in the fridge for weeks, a pair of freshly laundered socks, and an orange. This seemed to do the

trick. Arthur's antidote was not the sweetest smelling medicine in the world, but at least it was now drinkable.

Arthur poured half a pint of this mixture into a tumbler and carried it through to the sitting room, where Frank was having his afternoon nap. He removed the newspaper from Frank's face and woke him up. "This'll do it," he said, proudly.

"What? Kill me?" replied Frank, eyeing the foul, pink liquid with caution.

"This is the cure!" replied Arthur. "Guaranteed to sweep the cobwebs from your mind and to pump a zest for life through your tired limbs."

"I think I'd rather die," whinged Frank.

"You will if you don't drink it," said Arthur tetchily. "I've spent the whole afternoon making that for you. Go on, don't be such a baby!" Frank did not like being called a baby by his younger brother, and Arthur knew it.

"Oh, all right," said Frank, when all he wanted to say was no. "Here goes!"

Frank's stomach gurgled as the tumbler inched its way towards his mouth. The back of his throat, in fearful anticipation of what it was about to taste, tightened so fast that Frank choked. His tongue leaked saliva like a tent leaks rainwater. . . And Arthur's horrible antidote crept ever closer to Frank's lips. Then, suddenly, Frank screwed up his eyes, held his nose and poured the whole half pint down in one gulp. It hit the bottom of his stomach like a water bomb. POW!

Frank did not move a muscle. His face remained scrunched up like a walnut.

Arthur was waiting eagerly for a reaction.

Suddenly, it came! "Aaaaaaargh!" screamed Frank.

"It's worked!" shouted Arthur.

"It's burnt my tongue, you idiot!" yelled his elder brother. Frank made an undignified dash for the kitchen sink and plunged his mouth underneath the tap. As water gushed out from between his lips, he glowered at Arthur. "You goatbrain!" he said, in a definitive-sort-of-way. And that was the end of that.

"I've got another idea," said Arthur, as he chased Frank back into the sitting room.

"Well, I don't want to hear it!" snapped Frank.

"No, this one will work . . . I think," muttered Arthur, who was determined not to be beaten. "What I do, you see, is I turn all the clocks in the house back fifty-four years, to a few minutes before Old Ma McCracken gave you that boiled sweet. Only, this time, you don't eat it, and none of this will ever happen." Even as he was speaking, Arthur was thinking to himself how stupid this plan sounded.

"And just how long do you think it will take for you to turn all the clocks in this house back fifty-four years?" sneered Frank.

"Ten minutes?" proffered Arthur.

"I'd say, more in the region of fifty-four years!" said Frank. "Forget it, Arthur. Nice try. We are never going to find a cure. I'm going to die in three weeks' time and there's nothing you or I can do about it! Look, I don't like it any more than you do, but that's how it is."

There was a long silence. Frank and Arthur were both feeling sad. They had tried their best, but it just hadn't been good enough.

Arthur forced a weak smile. "Still," he said trying to sound cheerful, "look on the bright side."

"What bright side?" bemoaned Frank.

"Well, it's not every boy who has a

birthday every day of his life, is it?" said Arthur. But Frank was not amused, and Arthur took comfort from sucking his thumb in an upside-down position on the sofa.

Frank turned on the television.

CHAPTER 14

Those Glamorous Grannies

"Ladies and gentlemen!" declaimed the moustachioed man with sparkling white teeth and a tinsel suit. "Halibut Television, in association with Everlast Strongbone Corsets and Surgical Appliances, are proud to bring you, from the Mega Ballroom, in the heart of fabulous Birmingham, the glittering finale to the competition which has had the nation on the edge of its seat. Who will win this year's coveted crown? Who will be the United Kingdom's most Glamorous Granny?!"

The band struck up a slushy version of "When I'm Sixty-Four", and Frank and Arthur sighed. Of all the television programmes, in all of the world, they just *had* to be watching this one, didn't they!

The Mega Ballroom in Birmingham was an enormous room, topped by three hundred crystal chandeliers. At one end, there was a stage, on which the Glamorous Granny Compère, Bobby Sox, was cracking jokes and burbling inanely at the nearly rich and nearly famous in the audience. It was a night of a hundred stars. Celebrities from the four corners of Solihull were there, dressed up to the nines in their hand-me-down dinner jackets and black velour evening gowns.

Frank and Arthur started to suspect that something might be afoot, when Bobby Sox explained how the contest would be decided.

"We are looking," he said, "for the granny with the mostest! Our finalists will be judged on personality, on beauty, on charm, and on how they fare in our three special categories. Category number one: Who can leave the most lipstick smeared around a child's face after a long, sloppy, wet kiss.

Category number two: Who can scrub a child's face cleanest with nothing but a pocket handkerchief and a mouthful of wholesome, honest to goodness spit. And category number three: Who can give away the most boiled sweets in just five short minutes!"

Frank was dumbstruck. Old Ma McCracken would excel at all three categories. After all, she had had a lot of practice!

"So what?" said Arthur. "What can she do even if she does win?"

"She'll be the most famous granny in the country," stated Frank.

Arthur pondered this one long and hard. First the right way up and then upside down. It made little difference. He could still not see the relevance.

"People from all over will want to meet her," explained Frank. "She'll be asked to open fêtes, and kiss babies, and cut bits of ribbon outside supermarkets. She will be a celebrity."

"Will she really kiss babies?" asked Arthur.

"Of course," said Frank. "That's what celebrities do best!"

"Oh, dear," said Arthur. "That doesn't sound so good, does it?"

The brothers' worried faces said it all. It was a horrible prospect.

"Let's just hope she doesn't win, then," said Frank finally, turning his attention back to the competition.

Bobby Sox was in the middle of a joke about a granny and her false teeth when the picture suddenly cut backstage. Frank and Arthur could see The Dreaded Lurgie mingling with the other contestants. What a mixed bunch they were. Fat grannies, thin grannies, short grannies and long grannies. Grannies with little, round spectacles, grannies with shawls, and grannies with tiny, fat, snuffling dogs. Smiling grannies, serious grannies, young grannies, sporty grannies, rich grannies, poor grannies, smart grannies and grannies who looked as if they had just been dragged through a hedge backwards. Even though these grannies were on television, Frank and Arthur could smell that distinctive aroma of carbolic soap and home baking, that familiar, comforting scent of small dogs and mothballs! It was an extraordinary experience. Not least, because Old Ma McCracken counted herself amongst their number, and old witches do not make good grannies.

She was dressed up like a six-year-old girl in her best party dress. She had dyed her hair carrot red, and it bounced over her eyes and ears in long, springy ringlets. Her dress was made out of pink satin and trimmed with streamers of cheap white lace. It was too tight and too short. Her podgy white arms flopped out over the edges of the bodice and wobbled about like lumps of banana blancmange. The bottom of her

dress stopped just above her knees and showed off her legs to terrible effect. Over her surgical stockings, which she wore to constrict her varicose veins, Old Ma McCracken had slipped on a pair of royal blue tights embroidered with gold and silver stars. The tights were three sizes too big and hung in ungainly wrinkles around her knees and ankles. She had squeezed her feet into a pair of white high-heeled shoes swagged with cheap gold chains. She wasn't quite mutton dressed as lamb; she was more pig dressed as piglet.

"And the granny looked at the empty glass by the side of her bed and said, 'I thought that glass of water had more bite than usual!'" Bobby Sox reached the punchline to his joke. He waited for the laugh, but nobody in the audience had found it funny. Bobby tried to explain. "She'd drunk her false teeth, you see!" Still nobody laughed, so Bobby laughed for them. "Anyway," he continued, his smile unbroken, "now it's time to meet the contestants who are competing for this year's Glamorous Granny award!" The band played a fanfare and the audience applauded, because a man wearing headphones had told them to.

"And you are, my darling?"

"Ethel Baker," said the first contestant.

"From?"

"Basingstoke," giggled Ethel. "I'm a little bit nervous!"

"And so you should be, Ethel, wearing an embarrassing dress like that," Bobby joked. The audience did laugh this time, and Ethel blushed. "So what are your ambitions, Ethel, my dear?"

"I want to knit a scarf for my grandson, Toby, by Christmas," replied Ethel.

"What? No stunt flying on the wings of an aeroplane? No last minute trips around the world before you die?" roared Bobby.

"No," said Ethel meekly, "just the scarf." Bobby laughed some more and wished Ethel the very best of luck.

"Well that's a granny for you," he quipped, as Ethel disappeared in tears, and the next contestant appeared from behind the curtains.

She was a large lady with a chest like a mantelpiece. Arthur suggested that she had sneaked her grandchildren in with her, by stuffing them up her jumper.

"Don't be so rude!" said Nora, who had just sat down in front of the television to watch her Aunt Angina. "You can't judge a book by its cover. She may look like a bulldozer, but I'm sure she's as sweet as pie."

"My name is Brunhilde," boomed the granny with the mantelpiece, "and I like to take long walks and swim completely naked in icy fish ponds. I am also a taxi driver in my spare time and enjoy *not* picking passengers up when they want me to!" Bobby Sox was speechless.

Arthur and Frank put their heads in their hands. With opposition like this, there was a very real chance that Old Ma McCracken might win!

Their concern increased as they watched the next three contestants. One had a glass eye, which got stuck whenever she stared at the camera. It made her look like a demented axe-murderer, which did not endear her to the judges. The second had a tattoo on her neck saying "I love sailors", and a gold tooth at the front of her mouth with a diamond set in it. The third was dressed as a nun, and had quite obviously lost her marbles some years back.

However, when Old Ma McCracken appeared, as one of the last contestants, she knew that she had a fight on her hands. Two of the grannies who had gone before her had stood head and shoulders above the rest; Tilda Stamford from Chorley Wood, who had one hundred and forty-three grandchildren and knew each of them by name, and Francesca Rosebud from Mold, who ran Marathons and was the curator of the world's largest Dolls' Museum. One of them was tipped for the prize.

Nora crossed her fingers and sent up a silent prayer for her aunt to triumph.

Frank and Arthur crossed everything in sight, in the hope that The Dreaded Lurgie would give herself away, and reveal herself as the nasty witch that she undoubtedly was.

No such luck.

Old Ma McCracken had prepared herself impeccably. "Before we start, Bobby – I can call you Bobby, can't I? – may I say how handsome you are looking tonight," said

Ma McCracken, before Bobby Sox had even opened his mouth. "You do know that you are my favourite television personality. It is such an honour to be standing up here with you tonight. I'm sorry. You were saying?"

Bobby launched into his prepared questions. "And you are?"

"Mrs McCracken, but you can call me Angina."

"That's a very unusual name," observed Bobby.

"That's because I am a very unusual

person," replied Old Ma McCracken. "By the way, you've lost a button on your jacket. Remind me, after the show, and I'll sew it back on for you."

The audience loved her. Here at last was a granny behaving like a granny. And there was no stopping her.

"Bobby dear, you don't mind if I just say a wee hello to my two grandchildren, do you?"

Frank leapt up off the sofa. "She hasn't got

any grandchildren! She's lying!" he shouted.

"Sit down, Frank," said Nora. "Aunt Angina never lies. Besides, she wouldn't be allowed to enter the competition if she didn't have grandchildren."

"Frank and Arthur," said Old Ma McCracken.

"That's us!" yelled Arthur. "She's using our names!"

"Sssh!" ordered Nora. "I'm trying to listen. Isn't she beautiful?"

"Frank and Arthur," continued Old Ma McCracken. "My very special grandchildren. The two most important wee people in my life." Her voice was starting to crack, just as it had done at the public meeting.

"She's going to cry again!" shouted Arthur. "She's trying to trick the judges byplaying on their sympathy, and they don't know it!"

"My grandchildren have the faces of angels, Bobby." The old witch was on a roll. Her bottom lip had started to quiver. "Their hearts are so pure, it makes me weep. It's for them, and them alone, I want to win tonight. I *have* to win tonight! You see, Bobby, their mother, my daughter, was tragically killed last week in a car crash, and now the poor wee orphans have only me to turn to. I forgot to mention that their father's in prison. And I love them, Bobby. I love them so much that it hurts just to talk about them. But I must, for their sakes. Frank and Arthur, if you're watching, I love you, darlings. Stay safe until granny comes home. Don't miss me too much. I'm doing this for you . . . hoo . . . hoo . . . hoo." The tears rolled down Old Ma McCracken's face.

The audience were crying too. Even Bobby Sox had to dab his eyes with the sequins on the back of his sleeve.

Frank and Arthur were beside themselves with fury. "It's all lies," they shouted at the screen. "She's a fake! Surely *you* must know that, Nora. She's your family. You know that she hasn't got any grandchildren. She hasn't even got a daughter!"

But Nora was seeing her distant aunt through different eyes now, with renewed

admiration for a personal tragedy so nobly born. "I only know what Aunt Angina tells me about herself," she intoned, lovingly. "Why should she lie about having a daughter?"

"She's duped you along with the rest of them," insisted Frank.

"You know what your problem is, don't you?" said Nora.

Frank and Arthur didn't bother to answer, because they knew they were going to be told, anyway.

"Neither of you believe in the essential goodness of human nature. You should *forgive* my Aunt Angina for any wrongs she may have done to you in the past, not persecute her. Deep down inside she means no harm."

164

Frank and Arthur smiled, nodded their heads and accepted that Nora could no longer be trusted. Her colours were now pinned firmly to their opponent's mast!

After Old Ma McCracken's shameless performance, there was no more contest. The judges were captivated. The result was a foregone conclusion. They rated her lipsticky kisses as "slimed to perfection". Her spittle and handkerchief routine wiped the floor with her competitors, and her boiled sweets tasted so tum-dumplingly good that the judges awarded her top marks, and then added on a few more besides. She, quite literally, *stole* the show.

The crowning ceremony was awash with emotion. Tears flowed like tapwater, and hugs and kisses were handed round like jellies at a chimpanzee's tea party. Old Ma McCracken wore her crown with pride, and clasped the victor's trophy close to her heart. It was a magnificent bronze sculpture of a long piece of knitting on a rocking chair.

Bobby Sox pecked her on the cheek and announced to the world just exactly what she had won. "As reigning United Kingdom

Glamorous Granny of the Year," he sparkled, "Angina McCracken will be going on a nationwide, whistle-stop tour in the Glam–Gran–Charabanc to spread her own, very special, magic granny–formula to every lucky child in the country."

"No," shouted Arthur. "They mustn't let her! Frank, don't you see, THAT'S why she entered the competition. She's going for the jackpot! A boiled sweet for every single child in the country!"

But Bobby Sox had not finished. "So get out there, kids, and find her! She'll be there with a kiss, a wipe and an extra special sweetie for everyone. In twenty-three days, her tour will culminate in a party, the biggest party ever held, at Humptys, the world famous toy shop in London. No child should miss it! It's going to be the biggest and best free jamboree since jamborees began. There'll be cakes and conjurers and clowns, and crates and crates of toys and, of course, this lady – this dear, sweet, kindly old lady, dispensing her boiled sweets as only she knows how. Darling," he said to Old Ma

McCracken, taking her hand, and kissing her warty fingers, "we love you! Ladies and Gentlemen, I give you, Angina McCracken, our Glamorous Granny of the Year!"

There was mayhem. The audience rose as one, and applauded wildly. They stamped their feet, they banged their seats, they cheered and set off fireworks.

Old Ma McCracken bowed her head with mock humility, and laughed up the sleeve of her hired dress. "Come, little children," she whispered to herself. "Come to Granny McCracken, and see what surprises I've got in store for you!" Her eyes flashed and her teeth clicked in the roof of her mouth.

Frank and Arthur's worst fears were confirmed. The Dreaded Lurgie had won. She had been given a golden bus pass to Poison City. By the time she reached Humptys there would not be a child left in the country who was not dying of old age. In one hundred days, even the smallest babe in arms would be nothing but a pile of ancient bones, squashed under six foot of damp soil.

Frank and Arthur were the only ones

who understood the significance of her victory. They had to stop her. But how? Who could they tell? Who would believe them? Certainly not Nora, or the mayor, or the police chief, or their parents, who were still living the life of Riley in Barbados. In fact there was no one in their town who would give twopence for their story. They had no choice.

"We're on our own," said Arthur to Frank.

"Oh, dear," groaned Frank. "I was rather afraid you might say that."

CHAPTER 15

The Glam–Gran–Charabanc

The Glam–Gran Charabanc rolled out of Birmingham the very next day. Two hundred white doves of peace were released into the clear, blue sky, to mark Granny McCracken's departure. The mayor of Birmingham personally shook her hand, as photographers from every newspaper in the country fought to get the best picture. The Queen sent a telegram of congratulations to the nation's most Glamorous Granny, wishing her well for her forthcoming tour, and hoping that Granny McCracken might, one day, pay a visit to *her* grandchildren. The Prime Minister declared the day a national holiday.

The charabanc was a huge yellow bus with no roof. Hundreds of brightly coloured

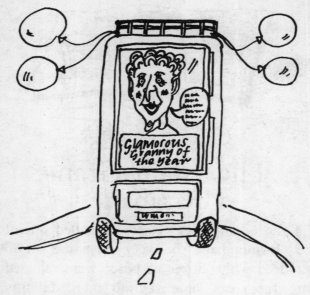

balloons fluttered from the rail which ran around the top deck, and a huge picture of Old Ma McCracken smiled at passers-by from the back of the bus. A speech bubble, coming out of her mouth, bore the message:

Come on kiddies,
Granny's here,
Her pocket full of treats.
She'll pick you up,
And dust you down,
And fill you full of sweets!

Old Ma McCracken sat on the top deck of the bus with a megaphone. She looked like an ancient admiral arriving home after a victorious sea battle. People lined the streets in their thousands. They waved, cheered and jostled each other, just to get a glimpse of their conquering hero. Of course, this was exactly what Old Ma McCracken had counted on. She waved back and generously showered the children with her irresistible boiled sweets.

"Be good children," she boomed, from

her majestic seat. "Eat them all up! And tell your friends that I'm here. I want to meet you all!"

The bus stopped every hour, for fifteen minutes. Then, Granny McCracken would descend into the crowd and dispense her blessing, in much the same way as a politician does during a General Election. Young children were passed across peoples' heads and handed to her. She would kiss them with her lipsticky lips and chuck them back. Boys with grazed knees and girls with scabby elbows approached to receive a kiss on their sore bits. Old Ma McCraken did not disappoint anyone. She slobbered over every child along her route, and poisoned them all.

Sometimes she liked to go walkabout into a shopping precinct or busy park. Bodyguards, assigned to their task by the sponsors of the competition, went with her at all times. They made sure that she was not bumped or knocked over by the huge crowds, and they gave her the space she needed to practise her evil magic.

In Southampton, a little girl fought her way

through the police cordon and presented the old witch with a bunch of freshly picked daffodils. "I picked them myself," said the little girl, proudly.

"Did you, my dear?" beamed Old Ma McCracken, bending down to stroke the little girl's soft, blonde hair. "What a pretty little girl you are. Have you cleaned your ears today?"

"Not today, no."

Old Ma McCracken removed her handkerchief from the sleeve of her dress. She spat on one corner, and beckoned the little girl closer. "Good little girls always clean their ears," she chastised. "At least once a day." Then she wrapped the handkerchief around her little finger and wiggled it around inside the little girl's ear.

The crowd loved to watch her work, and they broke into a spontaneous shout of "Three cheers for Granny McCracken!"

"There," said the world's most popular granny, removing her finger from the reddened ear. "That should have loosened things up a bit."

"Pardon?" said the little girl, who now could not hear a thing.

But Old Ma McCracken did not reply, because she had wandered off into the crowd, looking for fresh victims. "What a brilliant new way to infect the children," she thought to herself, "by packing the Lurgie in through the lughole. I must remember to use that one again."

In Norwich, she met a troop of Boy Scouts. "Such dirty knees," she gasped. They had been crawling through a forest, collecting firewood. "On your backs! Come along. Chop chop!" She made them lie down with their legs in the air, while she went along the row, spitting on their kneecaps and rubbing them clean with her handkerchief.

In Glasgow she was made "Very Special Guest of Honour" at Margaret Hardy's sixth birthday party. A great fuss was made of her as she arrived. Mr Hardy took her coat, Mrs Hardy offered her a large glass of sweet sherry, and Margaret asked her if she had brought her a present.

"Of course I have," said Old Ma McCracken, not hinting at what that present might be.

"Is it one of your special sweets?" shouted Margaret, jumping up and down with excitement.

"It is the most special of my special sweets. I was up all last night making it specially for you and your darling friends." Old Ma McCracken then produced a huge boiled sweet from underneath the coat of one of her bodyguards. It was so big that Margaret couldn't hold it. She had to roll it into the sitting room, where she and her friends used it as a sofa.

"Oh, you shouldn't have!" said Mrs Hardy, refilling Old Ma McCracken's sherry glass.

"Nonsense," replied Old Ma McCracken. "It was the least I could have done. I just want to make Margaret's sixth birthday a day she will never forget."

And the three adults smiled knowingly at each other, but Margaret's parents didn't know the half of it. They didn't have a clue what Old Ma McCracken *really* meant.

In Cardiff she gave a sweet to a fat boy named Gareth. He spat it out and told her it tasted like a cowpat. So, she took him into a corner and, when nobody was looking, clipped him round the ear. Then she asked him to try the sweet again.

"Delicious," he said, through his salty tears. "Absolutely delicious!"

And so the tour continued: Liverpool, Brighton, Totnes, Scarborough. From Land's End to John o'Groats, children flocked to see the granny to beat all grannies. She kissed them, and cuddled them. She fed them, and made them better. She put on a show that fooled the world.

Fooling everyone, that is, except Frank and Arthur.

"You know the Prime Minister," said Arthur.

"Not personally," replied the elder brother.

"Well, when he wants to convince the country that he's right and everyone else is wrong, how does he do it?"

"He lies through his teeth," said Frank, who was becoming wiser and wiser with each passing year.

"Yes, but how?"

"How does anyone lie?" asked Frank.

"By making it sound like they're telling the truth?"

"Exactly! And the best way to do that," continued Frank, who was starting to like the sound of his own voice, "is to produce tons of facts and figures to support your side of the argument."

"You mean, get things out of books, which say you're right?" Arthur was struggling hard to keep up.

Frank nodded. "Why do you want to know?" he asked.

"Because, if I can find something in a book which proves that Old Ma McCracken is a witch," explained Arthur, "then, everyone will have to believe me."

"Fat chance!" sneered Frank.

"Thanks for your support," Arthur said, crossing his arms and legs, and settling in for a jolly good think.

CHAPTER 16

Dead Flowers

The Snoggle Spots had gripped the nation's children by the dewlaps. Eminent physicians watched with alarm as tell-tale signs of premature ageing appeared all over the country. Grey hair and sensible shoes proliferated in the inner cities. Comfortable cardies and fat dogs with matchstick legs dominated the provincial towns. It was no coincidence that the spread of the disease corresponded exactly to the route taken by the Dreaded Lurgie's whistle-stop tour.

But nobody could see it.

When anyone asked her why she thought it was that the epidemic was following her around the country, she pointed out that *it* was not following her, she was following it. She saw herself as an angel of mercy, administering help and comfort to those suffering most. If she could spread a little happiness into the lives of those poor children who had been condemned to an early grave, was it not the least she could do?

This was prime twaddle, of course, but heroes and heroines can get away with just about anything if the public believe in their essential goodness. And, in Old Ma McCracken's case, the public did. They would have followed her to the edge of the world and jumped off if she had told them to, which is, of course, exactly where she was leading them.

She had made sure that almost every child in the country was now infected with the Snoggle Spots. Old age crept through the towns, streets and houses of the nation like poison through a network of veins. Imagine a leaf in Spring. A strong, supple green leaf, in the prime of its life. Imagine, then, the cold winds of Autumn. Imagine them coming early. Not in October, but in April. Just as the new leaf bursts tenderly into life, so it is attacked and battered by the cruel northerly winds. The leaf cannot withstand the attack. It shrivels and falls, and lies, forgotten, on top of a huge pile of leaves which have already died. Now imagine those leaves as children. This was the effect of The Dreaded Lurgie's black magic.

The streets were empty. The children were all indoors doing useful, grown-up things. Doing things that could not be put off till later. Things like mending a tap, or hemming a curtain. Either that, or they were just sitting there, waiting to die. There was very little else to do. Most schools had closed, because there was no one of the right age left to attend. The happy sound of squealing playground voices was a thing of the past.

In the new world created by Old Ma McCracken, the past became more important than the future. People stopped looking forward, because that way there was only death. Instead, they looked back. This is called nostalgia. As a result, the shops were full of records by Mel Torme and Andy Williams. Vast, tent-like knickers with elasticated waistbands suddenly became trendy, and children fought each other to

buy them. Trams reappeared on Brighton seafront. Ballroom dancing replaced disco dancing. Coach holidays to Morecombe-on-Sea grew in popularity, as package holidays to the Costa del Sol floundered. People flocked back to church on Sundays. Gambling casinos were closed down, and reopened as mega-leisure complexes catering for whist drives. And food rationing was reintroduced into the shops, because it made everyone feel more comfortable.

By looking back and never looking forward the country became a sadder place. Nobody played games, nobody took risks, nobody dared hope that things might get better. People simply accepted their lot, and lay down to die.

In a few weeks, the cemeteries of Britain would be jam-packed to overflowing.

CHAPTER 17

The Riddle

Frank did not want to go to the library with Arthur. Arthur didn't mind. When people reach seventy years old, they have the right to choose what they want to do. Besides, Frank had just been sent a new tartan travelling rug by an unknown benefactor. It had mysteriously appeared on the front doorstep that morning and Frank wanted to try it out in his favourite armchair. So Arthur left Frank contentedly asleep, with a cold cup of tea on the table in front of him.

The library was ever so quiet. Arthur's footsteps resounded like gunshots in a canyon as he walked towards the information desk in the centre of the entrance hall.

"Yes?" said a long, thin man, whose shirt collar was sticking up over the top of his jacket.

"Er . . . excuse me, but do you have a dictionary?" asked Arthur.

"We've got hundreds of dictionaries," replied the thin man, unhelpfully.

"Good," said Arthur. He didn't dare pluck up the courage to ask where he might find them, so he coughed instead.

The thin man let out an irritated squeak and stamped his tiny foot. "They're over there," he barked, waving his pencil around his head, and pointing in three different directions at once.

"Thank you," said Arthur, and he set off, not knowing where he was going.

He found a section called "Russian History", but when he browsed along the shelves, he couldn't see anything that remotely resembled a dictionary. He tried another section, "Home Cooking", and a third going under the enormously difficult-to-read name of "Para-Psychology", but neither was any good. He was just about to give up, when he saw a young woman, busy

putting books back on to a top shelf.

"Excuse me," said Arthur. He didn't have time to say anything else, because the woman screamed and slid down the sides of the step ladder, upon which she had been standing.

"Don't ever do that again," she said, nervously.

"What?" enquired Arthur.

"Speak to me!" she shouted. Then she ran off towards a door at the far end of the library. What a strange breed librarians were, thought Arthur. All he wanted to know was where the dictionaries were kept.

185

"Keep your thoughts down!" shouted the thin man from behind his desk. "There are people trying to read!"

"Sorry," muttered Arthur. He couldn't do anything right!

It crossed Arthur's mind, as he wandered down yet more corridors of books, that dictionaries were probably so rare and precious, that they couldn't be displayed on shelves. They had to be locked away in a safe where the sunlight could not destroy them. He was so busy thinking these thoughts, that he didn't notice that he had strolled into a gloomy corner of the library, which offered no further way forward. The sign over the shelves which blocked his way said: MYTHS AND LEGENDS.

"I bet there are no dictionaries in here, either," he moaned to himself, running his eye over the books just in case. A large book, in the middle of the shelf, caught his attention. It was the oldest book he had ever seen. It was bound in faded brown leather and had gold lettering embossed along the length of its spine. The letters were very faint, but when Arthur took a closer look, he could make out a word. It was the word he had been searching for: "*Dictionary*". It was part of a longer title: "A Dictionary of Weird Myths and Wonderful Legends." Arthur's eyes lit up!

He pulled it off the shelf and set it down on a reading table. The pages were enormous, and it took all of his strength to turn them. The book fell open with a deafening thunk. A cloud of dust billowed up from between the pages, and made Arthur cough.

"Ssssh!" snapped an old man, sitting next to him.

"Ssssh, yourself!" retaliated Arthur. He had had enough. He just wanted to be left alone, to study his dictionary in peace.

"And take your head off the chair!" came the thin man's voice again.

Arthur should have realized that you have to sit the right way up in a library. He swivelled his legs round and started to thumb through the pages. It wasn't long before he came across the word he was looking for.

LURGIE – Scottish derivation. Seldom used Scottish name. (Also see McLurgie)

*Noun — An irrational fear of all that is
young and bright. A hatred of new life.
Also, a disease causing premature old age —
(Slang) "The Dreaded Lurgie".*

That was all. It was interesting, but
nothing that Arthur did not already know.
He turned over a couple more pages in the
hope that the definition might continue
elsewhere, but it didn't. He had hoped that
he might find a simple recipe for a potion
to cure the disease, but, alas, that was not
the case.

It was then that Arthur noticed a
handwritten asterisk scratched on to the
page in blue ink. It was in the margin, just
above the word "LURGIE", and had a
number written next to it. The number
seven thousand and twenty eight. It seemed
an extraordinary thing for someone to
write in a dictionary. What did it mean?
Arthur racked his brains for an answer.
Then suddenly he had a thought. It was
probably a page number. He flicked through
the pages, until he found page seven
thousand and twenty eight, but, much to his
disappointment, there was nothing there.

It was the last page in the book, and it was blank.

He was just closing the book up, when he felt something lumpy underneath his fingers. The lump was in the cover. He opened the book again and noticed that the leather binding had been split along the seam and then restuck down. Someone had slipped a note into the cover of the dictionary. A secret note, which would only be found by a person looking up the word "LURGIE" and seeing the coded number. That person was Arthur. Maybe the note had something to do with the disease. Arthur could have speculated all day, but there was only one way of finding out.

He checked to see that no one was watching him, then slid his finger along the glued edge. The leather lifted easily, and, by feeling around inside the cover with his little finger, Arthur was able to extract a small piece of yellow paper. There was a note written on it, in blue ink.

I am dying from "The Dreaded Lurgie". I have only a few days left to live, and cannot, therefore, complete my research into its cure. What follows is all that I know. It holds the key to the formula which will rid the world of this foul plague, should it ever rear its ugly head again.

> *When East is West*
> *And bad is best.*
> *When water's dry*
> *And fish can cry.*
> *When hot is cold,*
> *A coward bold,*
> *When the outside's in the middle.*
> *Then you'll know*
> *In your big toe*
> *The answer to this riddle.*

Use my knowledge wisely, but be careful. Never forget the famous old Scottish saying: "Ich trim bore radley wurbunglydarn fook", which means, "Beware of old crones bearing boiled sweets."

YOU HAVE BEEN WARNED!

Anon
(London 1665)

This was it! Mr Anon, (whoever he was), had confirmed Arthur's theory. "Beware of old crones bearing boiled sweets". The written proof that he needed! Old Ma McCracken *was* that old crone. It was as plain as the nose on the end of Arthur's face. Now that he had this note, he could show it to anyone and they would have to believe him. He had got her! As for the riddle, Arthur would work it out later, with Frank's help.

He left the library, with the note tucked safely inside his pocket. As he passed the information desk, he thought, "Say your prayers, Dreaded Lurgie! Arthur's coming to get you!"

"Ssssh!" shouted the thin librarian. "Stop thinking!"

"Oh, shut up!" said Arthur.

And he went straight home.

CHAPTER 18

Eighty-three Years Long

It was day twenty-one of the Glamorous Granny Tour. Old Ma McCracken was stuck in Stockport, explaining to a group of infected youngsters why getting old was not really as bad as everyone made out.

"I'm nearly eighty," she declared, "and I'm still having the time of my life! There's plenty to look forward to in your latter years. You'll have families and grandchildren, and homes of your own."

"But we'll be dead in just over two months," said a boy with a large, pulsating boil in the middle of his forehead.

"That's true," replied Old Ma McCracken, clearing her throat, and spitting on the floor, "but you mustn't be negative.

Sixty days is sixty days. You can do a lot in that time."

"Like what?" came a voice from the back.

"Go three quarters of the way round the world. Nearly build a go-kart. You could start a business and pass it on to your children."

"But we can't have children," shouted the voice from the back again. "That takes nine months and we've only got sixty days."

"Oh, dear!" lied Old Ma McCracken. "That is a terrible shame. Children, you know, are one of life's greatest blessings!" She stifled a laugh, by turning it into a yawn. "I'm most terribly sorry, children, but I must away. I've got this jamboree at Humptys in a couple of days, and, tomorrow. . . Well, I don't like to boast, but I am having tea with the Queen and her grandchildren at Windsor Castle. I need my beauty sleep."

"You can say that again!" muttered the boy with the boil on his forehead.

Old Ma McCracken chose to ignore this remark. The boy would be dead soon, anyway.

Frank, meanwhile, was celebrating his

eighty-third birthday. Nora had bought him a bath chair with Old Ma McCracken's money.

"See how generous my aunt is!" eulogized the old woman's besotted niece. "You won't have guessed, but she bought you that travel rug as well. She didn't want you to think that she was handing out charity, so she sent it anonymously."

"She knew we wouldn't accept it," muttered Arthur to himself. "She's just being nice to stop people realizing that she's horrible."

Frank had learned never to look a gift horse in the mouth and had accepted the bath chair gratefully. It was not the most exciting present in the world, but it was practical.

"You know it's funny," muttered Frank, sucking on his gums, (his teeth had fallen out the week before), "but as the years pass, I find it increasingly difficult to remember how old I am."

"YOU ARE EIGHTY-THREE!" shouted Arthur, who had raised his voice to compensate for Frank's partial deafness. "Aren't you going to open my present?"

"No," said Frank.

"Charming!" replied Arthur.

"I'm not eighty-three. I'm eighty-two!"

Arthur raised his eyebrows. "You're eighty-three," he repeated, pushing his present on to Frank's lap.

"What is it?" asked Frank, looking at the envelope.

"It's an elephant," said Arthur. "Just open it and see." But Frank just sat there and smiled, instead.

Arthur was fed up with waiting. "Oh, give it here," he said. He took the envelope from Frank and tore it open.

"It's a piece of yellow paper," muttered Frank, disappointedly.

"It's not just any old piece of paper. I found it in the library. Read it!"

"I can't. I need my reading glasses," said Frank. "I've put them down somewhere, and for the life of me I can't remember where."

"They're on the end of your nose," said Arthur, "where you always keep them."

Frank grunted in a grumpy sort of I-knew-that-all-along way, and read his present.

"I'll tell you what this is," Frank said at last, folding up the piece of paper, neatly, on his lap.

"What?" said Arthur. He had known all along that Frank would be able to work the riddle out. After all, Frank was cleverer than he was when they were almost the same age. At eighty-three he must be brilliant.

"It's a riddle."

"Well, of course it's a riddle!" exploded Arthur. "But what does it mean?!"

"Haven't the foggiest," said Frank. "Is it important?"

"Oh, no," snorted Arthur. "It's only the *only* cure in the known Universe for the Snoggle Spots, that's all!"

"So it *is* important?" Frank replied, missing the point of his brother's sarcasm entirely.

Arthur gritted his teeth and just managed to stop himself from boxing Frank's ears. Instead, he read the riddle out loud, slowly and deliberately, so that his stupid brother could follow every word.

> *"When East is West*
> *And bad is best.*
> *When water's dry*
> *And fish can cry.*
> *When hot is cold,*
> *A coward bold,*
> *When the outside's in the middle.*
> *Then you'll know*
> *In your big toe*
> *The answer to this riddle.*

Now, what do you think it means?" he asked, for the second time.

"Well, East is never West," replied Frank, "and, unless I'm very much mistaken, water is never dry."

"Yes, I'd worked that out for myself, actually," said Arthur. "Do you think we should be looking for some dry water, then?"

"And a coward is never bold, and the outside of something can't possibly be in the middle."

"Frank," Arthur said, with a hint of annoyance in his voice, "I *can* read! But WHAT DOES IT MEAN?"

"Ahhhh. . ." mused Frank. "That is a very good question. . ."

But Arthur was never to hear Frank's answer, because, quite suddenly, Frank's eyelids slammed shut, his head slumped forward on to his chest, and his top lip vibrated like the skin of a kettle drum, as a huge, rattling snore shook the spectacles off the end of his nose.

It was quite obvious to Arthur that the riddle would remain unsolved unless he took matters into his own hands. Perhaps it would start to make sense if he could find out exactly what it was that Old Ma McCracken had put into her magic potion. There was only one way of finding that out. Frank and he would have to break into her house the next day.

He woke Frank up to explain his plan, but Frank was not as enthusiastic as Arthur had hoped. He did, however, agree to go along with it, so long as Arthur promised to leave him alone, for the time being, and let him sleep. Arthur agreed, reluctantly, and went and hung upside down from his parallel bars.

Frank did not sleep at all that night. It was not that he was over-excited at the prospect of his eighty-fourth birthday the following day, it was just that he was scared. Scared of what The Dreaded Lurgie might do to him and Arthur, if she caught them sneaking through her drawers.

CHAPTER 19

Royal Jelly

The Queen was in her parlour, counting out chocolate money for her grandchildren, when the butler came in.

"Granny McCracken!" he announced, in a voice so deep that it shook a huge, green emerald out of her crown.

"Hoorah!" shouted the grandchildren.

"Show her in," said the Queen.

Old Ma McCracken shuffled into the room and curtseyed as low as her corsets would allow. She had a basket of sweets over her arm, which she put down to shake the Queen's hand.

"One is delighted to meet you," squeaked the Queen.

"As is one, too," replied Britain's most

Glamorous Granny, getting her words in a twist. "These must be your beautiful grandchildren?"

"Indeed, them is," said the Queen. This word twisting thing was catching.

"Come and have a cuddle," smiled Old Ma McCracken. She knelt down on the floor and opened her arms wide to the children, as a scorpion might extend her pincers.

Arthur was struggling with Frank's bath chair. "Did you have to bring this?" he whispered, as he bumped Frank over the front step. He was terrified that the clanking might alert Nora to their expedition. She was in the kitchen cooking rock cakes and had expressly asked the boys to help her.

"There's no point in having a bath chair if I'm not going to use it," replied Frank, testily.

"It would have been a lot simpler for you to walk. Old Ma McCracken's house is only next door!"

Arthur steered Frank along the pavement and stopped underneath the big, black iron gates. The security camera did not move. It

had obviously been switched off while Old
Ma McCracken was away. The first problem
was how to get through the locked gates,
especially now that Frank insisted on doing
everything in his bath chair.

"We could climb over," suggested
Arthur.

"With my knees?" moaned Frank.

"We could dig a tunnel, then."

Frank laughed, mockingly. "It would be
simpler to drop us over the wall by
parachute!"

"You could be right," said Arthur.

"Oh, don't be stupid!" said Frank. "Let's
go home."

Just then the postman turned the corner
of the street and came towards them.

"Morning," he said.

"Hello," said Arthur. An idea was forming in his mind. "Have you got any mail for Mrs McCracken?"

"Have I ever?" laughed the postman, swinging a large sack off his back. "This is all for her."

"Shall I take it in for you?" said Arthur, helpfully. "It would save you a trip."

"How will you get through the gates?" asked the postman. This was the tricky bit.

"Oh, same way as you do, I expect," Arthur said.

The postman grinned. "Thanks all the same," he said, "but it'll be quicker if I do it myself. It's a very heavy sack."

Arthur's heart sank. His plan had failed. The postman smiled, then gave the gates a push. They swung open easily and the postman walked up the path. Arthur stared, goggle-eyed with disbelief. How could he have been so stupid? The gates had been unlocked all the time!

The brothers waited on the pavement until the postman had delivered his letters and walked off down the street. Then they let themselves in through the gates. Arthur pushed the bath chair up to the side of the house, and jammed on the brake.

"Right," he said, helping Frank to his feet. "Let's look for an open window, or something."

"More jelly?" asked the Queen, handing the bowl to Old Ma McCracken.

"Thank you, your Majesty, but one is a tad full to bursting!"

"Very well, have a choccie biccie, then."

"Save them for the children," said Old Ma McCracken. "I could murder another cup of tea, though."

The Queen clapped her hands and four footmen skipped into the room. One was carrying a silver teapot; the second, a silver milk jug; the third, a silver sugar bowl; and the fourth, a pair of silver sugar tongs.

"Thank you ever so much," said Old Ma McCracken, as they poured her another cup of tea.

"One does so love a simple tea party," said the Queen. Then she added, by way of making idle chit-chat, "One is appalled by this terrible Snoggle Spots thing, don't you think?"

"Oh, appalled!" lied the Royal guest.

"And one is so terribly grateful for all the work you do to help our country's sick children," continued Her Majesty, playing right into Old Ma McCracken's hands.

"I do my best," said the old impostor, with just the right amount of humility.

"So, tell me, what makes you a better grandmother than oneself?"

"Oh, I'm sure that's not the case," said Old Ma McCracken, modestly. "My weakness has always been children, you see. All I'm trying to do, in my own wee way, is irreversibly to change their lives."

"To change their lives?"

"For the better, of course."

"Of course," said the Queen. "And you believe that kisses, wipes and boiled sweets are a good way to do it?"

"Undoubtedly, your Majesty."

"One is very interested by that. Might one try it, do you think?" Old Ma McCracken feigned disbelief.

"What? Your Majesty would like to give your grandchildren one of *my* boiled sweets?"

"If you think one can."

"But of course, your Majesty! It would be
my pleasure to watch you." Then she
uncovered her basket and gave the Queen a
handful of boiled sweets.

"Here children!" shouted the Queen.
"Come to one's grandmother!"

The children came running, like a pack
of corgis.

Frank and Arthur had found a way in. There was a coal hole round the back of Old Ma McCracken's house, which dropped straight into her cellar. Arthur had removed the cover and was trying to persuade Frank to jump down the hole.

"I'm not eight years old any more, you know," protested Frank.

"I'll go first," said Arthur, "and catch you." Frank snorted. "You'll drop me, you mean."

"All right then, stay up here and keep lookout, in case The Dreaded Lurgie arrives home unexpectedly."

"But it's cold up here," complained Frank.

Arthur looked at his watch. "We've got one hour," he said, trying desperately to control his urge to push Frank's bath chair into the rose bushes. "Old Ma McCracken will be returning home for an early night before the party at Humptys. If we don't go in now, we may never get another chance."

"I'll stay up here," said Frank. "Don't you worry about me." Then he added, as a homage to martyrdom, "There's only an outside chance that I'll die from hypothermia!"

As Arthur slid down the coal chute, he had serious doubts about the wisdom of this adventure. He hadn't got a clue what he was looking for, and what if he couldn't get out again? He landed with a squelch on something soft and furry. The cat screeched and shot up the cellar steps to safety. Unfortunately, it had forgotten that the door was locked. It banged its nose sharply against the wood and knocked itself out.

By the fading light which was trickling down the coal hole, Arthur could just see his way around the cellar. He found the freezer and opened it up. The interior light came on and helped him to see more clearly. Not that there was much to see. There was an empty cauldron, and a few burnt twigs on the floor beneath it. A couple of cardboard boxes and an old iron bedstead lay in a heap in one corner, and there were sticky cobwebs hanging everywhere. The air was filled with the dust which he had disturbed when he landed. But could he see a jar of sweets, a box of handkerchieves or a crate of lipsticks? No. Someone had had a very thorough clear up.

He found an old key hanging by the

cellar door, and discovered, to his surprise, that it fitted the lock. He turned it, and edged the door open. He was in Old Ma McCracken's hall. It was very dark, and smelled of cats. He didn't want to stay there any longer than he had to.

He decided to check each room in turn and started with the kitchen. There were all sorts of bottles and tins lying around on the table, but their labels confirmed that they contained nothing more dangerous than food well past its sell by date. In the sitting room he became suspicious of a metal bucket by the fireplace. It contained something pretty gunky and unpleasant. He was going to stick his finger into the gloopy substance and taste it, when he suddenly realized what it was. It was Old Ma McCracken's spittoon and he dropped it like a hot potato. Upstairs, he fared no better. The bathroom was damp and musty. Large, brown mushrooms grew between the wall tiles, and their spores hung in the air like tiny space rockets.

"She might make her poison out of these mushrooms," thought Arthur, taking a firm grip on the biggest one. He gave it a sharp tug. The mushroom came off the wall with

surprising ease, but, unfortunately, so did the tiles. He was sent spinning backwards and landed bottom-down in the loo. Now *he* was damp and musty, and the mushroom was squashed. Arthur left the bathroom with nothing more to show for his visit than a wet seat to his trousers.

The last room he entered was her bedroom. What a mess! It was packed with all sorts of junk. Boxes, trunks, suitcases and plastic carrier bags were piled to the ceiling. Their contents spilled out into the room the way lava flows down the side of a volcano. Arthur nearly cried. He didn't know where to start looking.

"They seem to love them," said the Queen, as she handed yet another boiled sweet to yet another grandchild. She held the sweets in the centre of her hand, with her palm flat, and forced them into the children's mouths, just as one would feed a horse. "Isn't this fun!" she guffawed.

"Aye!" agreed Old Ma McCracken. "It's the best fun I've had in ages!"

What a wicked old lady she was. Now, even

the royal grandchildren had caught the Snoggle Spots, and, what is worse, they had been given them by the Queen of England herself!

Old Ma McCracken stood up and curtseyed. "Your Majesty, if you will excuse me. Tomorrow it's Humptys, and I really must get some sleep. It has been a delight."

"One has thought much the same oneself! We thank you, dear Granny McCracken, for being so kind and cuddly, and I speak for oneself, when I say that you make the most delicious boiled sweets that I have ever tasted."

Old Ma McCracken caught her breath sharply. So sharply, in fact, that her teeth fell out! The Queen was not meant to eat one of her boiled sweets! "*You've* tasted one of my sweets, your Majesty?" she said.

"Yes. It was yummy-scrummy," said the Queen, licking her lips.

"And how do you feel? Any different?" enquired Old Ma McCracken, searching the Queen's face for any new signs of ageing.

"Tired, if you must know," replied the Queen. "I think it must be time for the royal afternoon nap! Good-day, Granny

McCracken. Keep up the good work! You may tell Nannies Charlotte, Ruth, Louisa, Helen, Elspet and Flo to come in on your way out. Goodbye." Old Ma McCracken curtseyed once more, then scuttled off, as fast as she could, for home.

Arthur, meanwhile, was still sifting through the junk in Old Ma McCracken's bedroom. He had found all sorts of things. Piles of dirty clothes, bundles of old letters, and tea chests crammed with broken china, but nothing resembling a poisonous potion. It was all rather depressing. He sat down on top of a black, plastic bin liner full of old shoes and looked at his watch.

"Oh, my goodness!" he yelled. He had been rummaging for over two hours! Old Ma McCracken might return at any moment!

He dashed out of the bedroom at breakneck speed, leapt across the landing, and slid down the bannisters. How could he be so stupid as to not notice the time! He ran back along the hall and, in the darkness, found the handle to the cellar door. He tugged it open, and stepped through. Then he relocked the door, hung the key back on its nail, went down the cellar steps, shut the lid of the freezer and hurried over to the bottom of the coal chute.

"Frank!" he shouted. "Frank! Help me up!"

There was no reply. "Frank!" Still, nothing. "Frank, are you asleep?" he bellowed, at the top of his voice.

"Of course not," came the reply from the other end of the coal hole. "It's too cold to go to sleep!"

"I'm late!" Arthur said, urgently. "The Dreaded Lurgie may come back at any moment! You've got to help me get up this chute!" There was a strange rustling from above, followed by the creak of newly plaited wicker. Then, suddenly, Frank's tartan rug flopped down through the coal hole and hung in the air, just above Arthur's right hand.

"Grab the other end of this," shouted Frank, "and pull yourself up."

Arthur did as he was told.

Thirty seconds later, Arthur had replaced the coal hole cover, and was pushing his elderly brother back through the big iron gates.

"Well," said Frank. "Did you find anything?"

"Nothing, I'm afraid," replied Arthur. "Whatever it is that she uses to poison us children, she doesn't leave it lying around the house. She must keep it on her."

"Oh," said Frank, who was looking rather sad. "So, that's it then?"

"No, it's not," Arthur said, with a grin. "We're going back in there later tonight, when Old Ma McCracken's asleep!"

There was a smell of burning rock cakes as Frank and Arthur slipped quietly through their front door.

"Where do you think you've been?" said

216

Nora's cross voice. She was standing behind the door with a rolling pin.

"We went for a spin in the park. Lost track of the time. Sorry!" fibbed Arthur, quickly.

"Thanks to you," seethed Nora, "my rock cakes are a disaster!" She was really upset. "Now get into the kitchen – both of you – and scrape the black bits off your mother's pans!"

The boys were grateful to get off so lightly and set about the washing up with such eagerness that Nora secretly forgave them.

As Arthur splashed suds up and down the wall and Frank dried, a long, black, stretch-limousine, with smoked glass windows, purred up the street, stopped outside Old Ma McCracken's house, and switched off its lights. The Dreaded Lurgie was back!

CHAPTER 20

Mrs McCracken's Bloomers

Frank and Arthur barely had time to go to bed before they had to get up again. It was midnight. The wind rattled their bedroom window, and drove the rain horizontally down the street.

"Typical," thought Frank. "I'm eighty-four years old, I've got a weak chest, arthritic knees, bad circulation in my feet, and now I am about to spend the night sitting in a witch's garden, in the middle of the wettest, coldest storm that this country has ever suffered!"

"Looking forward to it?" piped up Arthur.

"If one can look forward to certain death! Yes, I'm ecstatic at the prospect of breaking

into Old Ma McCracken's house," moaned Frank.

"So am I!" said Arthur, unhooking his feet from the parallel bars, dropping down on to his hands, and picking up his clothes.

Old Ma McCracken had only just gone to bed. She had been in a terrible mood all night. Cats had been spinning across her bedroom and smacking into the walls, like plates in a Greek Taverna. She had been cursing herself for allowing the Queen to eat a boiled sweet. If Her Majesty was to die suddenly, in the middle of the night, it would ruin all of her plans. The Humptys' jamboree would be cancelled, and the few remaining children who had not yet received their deadly dose of poison would never turn up. It would only take a few healthy children to slip through her net and the country would be saved!

She had spat at herself in the mirror before climbing into bed. "That'll teach you, you feeble old woman. You crepitous old grutnol! Call yourself a Lurgie! You're a disgrace to the name! You should be boiled in oil and fed to the guzzling, goop-hopping, shim-scally-waggling monsters!"

Bizarre behaviour, I think you'll agree, but possibly not, when you consider that she was stark raving bonkers. Anyway, the point is, that she had finally gone to sleep. Frothing ever so slightly from the mouth, but asleep, nonetheless, which suited Frank and Arthur's purposes right down to the ground.

Arthur carried Frank downstairs and helped him into his bath chair. Then he put an umbrella in his hand and tucked the all-important travel rug over his knees.

"Ready?" he asked.

"No," said Frank.

"Good! Then, off we go!" said Arthur, ignoring his brother's feeble protestations.

They had decided against taking a torch, reasoning that a bright, flashing light might give them away. As a result, things were a little bit darker than they might have wished for. Apart from the large puddles on the pavement, the street was empty. Apart from the splattering of the rain on Frank's umbrella, it was silent, too. No hungry babies, crying for a bottle. No screaming children, waking from a nightmare. No noisy teenagers, partying until dawn. Only occasionally did the sound of a shovel shifting dirt rise above the silence, as the gravedigger prepared for a rush of work.

The iron gates were still unlocked. Arthur pushed Frank through and parked his bath chair by the coal hole.

"Are you sure it's safe?" Frank asked, for the umpteenth time that night.

"No," replied Arthur. "I'm sure it's unsafe, irresponsible and completely barmy, but I've got one major advantage over that old witch, and I'm relying on that to pull me through."

"What is it?" asked Frank.

"I can run faster than she can!" Arthur

shook Frank's hand and disappeared down the hole in the ground.

He knew his way around Old Ma McCracken's cellar this time, and went straight for the cellar door key. The wooden door creaked slightly as he opened it. He held his breath and stretched his ears to listen. Nothing stirred upstairs. Old Ma McCracken was asleep. He tiptoed along the dark hallway and reached the foot of the main staircase.

A pair of yellow eyes blinked in the darkness, and followed Arthur as he started to climb the stairs.

He held on to the bannisters with his left hand and put his right hand on the wall. If he pressed evenly on both sides at once, he found that he could lighten himself and reduce the risk of making a noise. If he trod on a cat, or made a floorboard creak now, he was dead.

As he reached the landing, Arthur heard a comforting sound, which raised his spirits. It was Old Ma McCracken's snoring. It consisted of two parts. A low, floppy-lipped rumbling, which built up like an approaching earthquake, and flattened out when she had sucked in more air than a vacuum cleaner. And a high-pitched whistle, which woke up the neighbourhood dogs and loosened the light brackets in her bedroom. It was lucky for Arthur that she was such a noisy sleeper. It meant that if he did knock anything over by mistake, she probably wouldn't hear it.

The bedroom door was slightly ajar. He could see the bulky shape of Old Ma McCracken asleep in her bed. A streetlamp shone through her threadbare curtains and threw a yellowish glow over her face. Arthur had never studied The Dreaded Lurgie's face in such detail before. He had never realized quite how ugly she really was.

For a start, she didn't have any hair. Her wig sat on a block by the side of her bed. It was full of curlers, and was obviously being prepared for the jamboree at Humptys later that day. Her teeth were lying on the floor. A marmalade cat was licking them clean. Her face, far from looking peaceful, was twisted into an angry snarl, and from the corners of her mouth flecks of spittle ran down her chin and gathered in the folds of skin around her neck. Without make-up, she

bore a frightening resemblance to a corpse.

Arthur could have stared at this extraordinary apparition all night, but there was work to be done. He located her handbag under the bed and sprang open the snake's head clasp. He had never seen such a mess. Everything had been hurled in, willy-nilly. It was the sort of bag where, if you plunged your hand into the middle of it, you could just as easily pull out a dead cockroach as a daily diary. Unfortunately, Arthur had no choice. He had to find her sweets, her handkerchief, her lipstick and, if possible, some of the poison, so that he could conduct an experiment on them when he got home.

He took a deep breath and shoved both hands into Old Ma McCracken's bag. It was not a pleasant experience. He couldn't tell what it was that he was touching, but, whatever it was, it made his flesh crawl. There were cold things, warm things, furry things and sharp things. Things with bits that squirmed, and stuff that squelched. Things that cracked, and puffed and scurried and split. And some things that were better left well alone. At last,

Arthur felt a sweet. He could tell it was one of Old Ma McCracken's boiled sweets because he recognized the wrapping. He took it out of the bag and slipped it into his pocket.

Arthur could not find a handkerchief or a lipstick in the bag, though, which puzzled him. Where would *he* hide his most treasured possession if he didn't want anyone to find it? In a drawer? Behind a picture? Under a rug? He looked around the room, until his eyes came to rest on the bed. "Of course," he muttered to himself. "Oh, dear! The witch has got them in bed with her!"

This was going to be tricky. Old Ma McCracken was still wearing her dayclothes, even though she was in bed. "A dirty slut", her mother had once called her, when she was fifteen, and "a dirty slut" she had remained. Unpleasant tasks call for brave hearts. Arthur would need to be brave if he was going to run his hands through her crumpled clothes and pick her pockets.

The bottom sheet felt crispy, like caramelized toffee, as Arthur slid his hands underneath the old woman's back. He was feeling for something lumpy. He moved his hands gently over her arms and down to her great, big, wobbling tummy. It felt as if he were frisking a hippopotamus. She snorted as he passed his hands over her bellybutton, and he froze. She blew out a long blast of stale breath and turned over. Her bottom was now firmly in the picture. There was nothing else for it, Arthur was going to have to rummage through her bloomers!

He touched them as one might touch a dead skunk – at arms' length. It was not a job he would have chosen to do, but it was one that had to be done, nonetheless. Arthur set to it, with all the enthusiasm of a fox handling furs in a fox fur factory. He ran his fingers down the shiny black material very gently, but he could feel nothing inside the left leg of her bloomers except for pound upon pound of hard, dimpled flesh. He transferred his attention to the right leg and was swiftly rewarded. Nestling in a small pocket just above her right knee, he felt the phial. The phial full of her evil potion. The phial which she had hidden away on that very first night. The only problem was that Arthur would have to slip his hand up the leg of her bloomers to reach it. This would require the utmost care and concentration!

He blew on his hands to warm them up, and gingerly stretched the knicker elastic which held her bloomers tightly around her knee. Then, ever so gently, he inched his hand up inside her underwear. For a moment he thought he had lost the phial, buried as it was amongst the swags of voluminous material, but at last, his little fingers touched the cold glass tube, and he grabbed it.

Unfortunately, as he withdrew his hand, he let go of the knicker elastic rather too quickly. It snapped back on to her podgy flesh with the force of a whip. She sat bolt upright in bed and screamed. Arthur took one look at Old Ma McCracken, rising from her pillow like a fearsome, blubbery sea monster, and fled.

As he slid down the bannisters, he could hear the old woman clambering out of bed, and screaming blue murder. "Help! Thief!" she cried. Her thick, elephantine legs thumped on the floor above Arthur's head, as he reached the cellar door.

He burst through the door like a tank. Nothing was going to stop him now!

Unfortunately, he was going just a little bit
too fast and he stumbled on the top step of
the cellar stairs. He fell forwards, crashed
down the wooden steps, and ended up in a
heap at the bottom. His first thought was
for the phial. Luckily, it wasn't broken, but
the cork had slipped out, and a small pool
of green liquid had spilled on to the cellar
floor. A sleepy-looking cat appeared out of
the gloom, gave Arthur a look of withering
disdain, and lapped up the liquid. The
effect was stupendous!

Within seconds, smoke started to pour

out of the cat's ears. Its fur fell out, its head started to shrink, and its skin began to sag until the poor creature looked like one big, pink wrinkle. Then the wrinkle crumbled, and fell away, leaving just a skeleton, which lurched forward, clattered to the ground and disintegrated. The cat had died from old age, in just under five seconds.

Arthur looked at the phial of green liquid in his hand. This was the stuff, all right! This was Old Ma McCracken's dastardly, magic potion! He replaced the cork, very carefully.

Suddenly, there was a crash in the hall. Old Ma McCracken had slipped on the hall rug and knocked over the umbrella stand. Arthur forgot about the pile of grey cat dust and stood up. The tartan rug was already hanging down through the coal hole.

"Quick! Pull me up!" he whispered loudly to Frank. Frank coughed to prove that he wasn't asleep. Then Arthur grabbed hold of the rug and disappeared up through the coal hole, just as Old Ma McCracken switched on the cellar lights.

She had missed him.

CHAPTER 21

A Race Against Time

Frank was exhausted when they finally got back to their bedroom.

"You must stay awake!" hissed Arthur, shaking his brother, roughly. "We must find a cure tonight. You may not be around tomorrow morning!"

"Can't I just sleep for a little bit?" complained Frank. His eyelids were extremely heavy. They kept trying to shut without him noticing.

Arthur propped two pillows behind Frank's back, which forced him to sit bolt upright.

"I'm going to mix an antidote," said Arthur.

"You tried that once before. It didn't work."

"I didn't have The Dreaded Lurgie's

231

potion before, did I?"

"Well, I shan't drink it!" Frank said. "Not if it burns my mouth again like the first one."

"It won't," stated Arthur.

"It will!"

"It won't," repeated Arthur.

"It might!"

"IT WON'T!" shouted Arthur, who was finding his elder brother's negative attitude incredibly frustrating. "I'm just going to get the tooth mug from the bathroom," he added, tiptoeing out of the room so as not to wake Nora.

Arthur poured a small amount of Old Ma McCracken's green potion into the bottom of the mug, and turned to his wizened old brother.

"I'm going to add things that you liked when you were eight," he said. "Things that you associate with being a child."

"Football boots," said Frank, grumpily.

"Don't be stupid. I can't dissolve football boots, and you certainly can't drink them! Think again!" Arthur was becoming quite bossy. "Let's start with your favourite foods."

"Sugar," said Frank, "and rice pudding. Strawberry jam, frozen peas, cherries, oranges *without* the pips, chicken curry and white bread."

"Good," said Arthur, more calmly, "now we're getting somewhere. The chicken curry might prove to be a problem, but I should be able to find the rest in the kitchen. While I'm away, try and think of anything other than food which you remember liking."

While Arthur was away, Frank did exactly that.

"Flowers," he declared, when Arthur returned from the kitchen, with his antidote. "I liked flowers when I was eight. And dogs. Not big dogs, because they were too big, but medium sized dogs, with wet noses and huge paws."

"I can get a flower from the front garden," said Arthur, "but as for the dog. . . Well, you can shoot me down in flames if I'm wrong, but I don't think I'll be able to fit a dog in this tooth mug!"

"I was just telling you what I liked," Frank said, defensively.

"What about comics?"

"What *about* comics?"

"We could shred the front page of the *Beano*, easily."

"OK," said Frank. "And my football cards."

"Right," said Arthur. "I'll see what I can do."

For the next half an hour, Arthur worked feverishly. He pummelled and pasted his antidote, adding all that Frank had requested, and a few more things besides (a can of Coca Cola, one Subbuteo soccer player with a broken neck, three coloured wax crayons and a daddy long legs, who happened to be in the wrong place at the wrong time). When he had finished, he had created a thick, soupy gunge in the bottom of his mug.

"Are you ready?" said Arthur.

"Yes," replied Frank.

"Then take a sip, and let's see what happens," Arthur said, handing the antidote to his brother. Frank shuddered, wrinkled up his nose and sipped a tiny drop. The effect was instantaneous and most dramatic.

His face creased up like an old leather

boot. His eyes slouched down his face, until they bobbled about on his cheek bones. His lips turned a faint shade of blue. His shoulders bowed and his head slumped forward on to his chest. Slowly, he raised the mug to his lips to take a second sip.

"STOP!" shouted Arthur. "Stop! It's not working. Drink another drop and you'll end up like that cat in Old Ma McCracken's cellar!"

The mug slipped from Frank's fingers and tumbled to the floor. "I'm sorry," said Arthur. "It's just making you older." Arthur put his arm around his brother's shoulder and kissed him on the forehead. "Don't worry," he said. "We'll find a cure before tomorrow. I know we will." Then he helped Frank into bed, leapt up on to his parallel bars, and hung upside down by his ankles in a seriously serious thinking position.

"You know what bugs me?" said Arthur, as he swung there in the darkness. "Why did you contract the Snoggle Spots, and I didn't? I mean, I know that Old Ma McCracken wiped your face, gave you a kiss and made you eat a boiled sweet, but she did the same to me and I'm all right." He

paused to think. "So, what is it that's different between you and me? What have I got that's special? What have I got that protects me from her magic potion?"

There was a long silence.

"Frank?"

But Frank was asleep.

CHAPTER 22

The Dream

Frank was still asleep when Arthur dropped down from his parallel bars the following morning. He flipped himself over into a standing position and leant over his brother to check that he was all right. He got the sort of shock that you only want to get once in a lifetime. Frank's breathing was very irregular. It came and went in short, shallow bursts. His lips were now dark blue and his fingers icy cold. Arthur was scared. He shouted for Nora, who came rushing into the bedroom wearing only her nightie.

"He's dying!" shrieked Arthur, forcing Old Ma McCracken's niece to look at Frank's ashen face. "You've got to do something!"

"We've already seen a doctor," said Nora,

who was confused by Frank's sudden deterioration. "What else can we do? Aunt Angina told me that there was nothing to worry about. Leave Frank alone, she told me, it's best not to interfere with the body's natural healing processes!"

"That's what she wanted you to believe," said Arthur. "It suited her purpose. She was lying! Phone my parents. Make them come home. Do something, please!"

Nora conceded with a nod of her head. Then she looked at Frank, lying motionless on the bed. "I didn't realize," she said pathetically. She left the room with her head hung in shame.

Arthur jumped on top of Frank and slapped his face.

"Wake up, Frank! Wake up," he cried. "Don't die now. You mustn't give in to it. Fight it, Frank! Frank!"

Frank opened one eye and tried to smile. "It's no good, Arthur," he said, in a tiny voice no louder than a baby bird's. "I'm too tired to carry on fighting. Let me sleep. Please, let me sleep."

"No, you can't. You mustn't!" yelled Arthur. "I had a dream, Frank, a most extraordinary dream. Wake up and listen."

Frank's hand slid across the bed cover and touched Arthur's arm. "I am listening, Arthur," he whispered. "Tell me your most extraordinary dream."

"I don't know what it means," Arthur said, "but I was in a world where everything was upside down. It was as if I was looking through a fairground mirror. Everything was the opposite to how it is here. People walked backwards down the street and said 'Hello' to passers-by, when what they meant was 'Goodbye'. Nobody wore clothes, except when they took a bath, and I saw a flock of sheep wearing dinner jackets. No wool, just man-made suits. If you went on a bus, you had to walk *down* the staircase to get *up* to the top. Aeroplanes flew under the sea, and boats sailed across the sky. It was madness. Can you imagine having the front door of your house on the third floor? It just didn't make sense. The sun shone and it was dark, but when the moon came out, the earth was flooded with light. Trees grew the wrong way up, with their roots at the top and their fruit buried underground, and the most bizarre thing I saw was this policeman. He reversed his panda car round a corner, with his wheels on the pavement, jumped out, threw a brick through a jeweller's window and stole a diamond necklace."

Frank had opened his eyes. "I don't know what it means, either," he said softly, "but I do know where I've heard something similar before."

"Where?" said Arthur.

"In that riddle you got from the library."

"You're brilliant!" whooped Arthur. "That's the missing link!"

Arthur hurried to fetch the piece of yellow paper from its secret hiding place in his piggy bank. Then he sat next to Frank on the bed and read it aloud.

"I am dying from 'The Dreaded Lurgie'. I have only a few days left to live, and cannot, therefore, complete my research into its cure. What follows is all that I know. It holds the key to the formula, which will rid the world of this foul plague, should it ever rear its ugly head again.

When East is West
And bad is best.
When water's dry

And fish can cry.
When hot is cold,
A coward bold,
When the outside's in the middle.
Then you'll know
In your big toe
The answer to this riddle."

Frank smiled. "You see," he said. "That's what your dream was trying to tell you. The cure has got something to do with opposites."

"Fish can't cry, then?" asked Arthur.

"I don't think so," replied Frank.

"But what does 'your big toe' mean? Surely, you would know the answer to the riddle in your brain. Your big toe's at the other end of your body. I haven't got a brain in my big toe."

"Unless. . ." muttered Frank.

"Unless, what?" said Arthur, leaning a little closer to his brother, so as not to miss a single word.

"Unless, your big toe was where your brain normally is."

"Between your ears?" said Arthur, who had still not grasped what Frank was driving at.

"No. At the top of your body, instead of at the bottom."

"But you'd have to stand on your head for that to be the case," said Arthur.

"Precisely," said Frank. "And what do you see if you stand on your head?"

"Everything's upside down," replied Arthur. He had clicked. "So, I didn't catch the Snoggle Spots, because I was standing on my head when she kissed me and gave me the sweet!"

"It's a possibility," said Frank.

"It's a very definite possibility!" repeated Arthur. Even as he spoke, another brilliant plan was forming in his head. As the plan grew, the smile on his face broadened to a huge, Cheshire cat-type grin. He grabbed hold of Frank's blankets and pulled them off the bed. "Come on!" he yelped. "Out! There's no time to lose. Come on, hurry up!"

"What are you doing?" asked Frank, who was cold and a little concerned by the mad glint in his brother's eye.

"I'm going to hang you upside down from the ceiling by your ankles!" shouted Arthur. He was so excited at solving the riddle, that his tiny feet would not stay still.

They jiggled and wiggled across the carpet like a couple of electric eels.

"But I'm too old to hang upside down!" protested Frank.

"Nonsense," said Arthur, helping Frank off the bed, "you're only eight years old. Where's your sense of adventure?"

"Take those ropes off me!" Frank said, as Arthur tied one end to Frank's ankles, and threw the other end up over the parallel bars. "You're not seriously going to string me up, are you?"

"You bet!" said Arthur. "It's going to work, Frank. It's going to work!"

Arthur needed all his strength to lift Frank off the ground. It took several hefty tugs on the rope and left Arthur quite red in the face.

"How does it feel?" Arthur asked his topsy-turvy brother.

"I think my head's going to burst," whined Frank. "Somebody's thumping on the inside of my skull with a sledgehammer!"

"You'll get used to it," said Arthur. He tied the rope to the door handle and sat down on Frank's bed to watch.

"What now?" said Frank.

"We wait," replied Arthur. "Isn't this exciting?"

Frank thought not.

As it happened, Frank and Arthur did not have to wait long.

After a couple of minutes, Frank compained that he had sand in his brain. "My head is full of the stuff!" he shouted. "It's coming out of my ears!" And it was! A tiny trickle of sand spilled out of the corner of each ear.

"It tickles!" yelled Frank. This was the first childish thing he had said for weeks.

"It's pouring out faster, now!" observed Arthur, catching some in the palm of his hand. "It really is sand, too!" He knew that this time he had cracked it. "How do your feet feel?"

"Sore," replied Frank.

"Well, they should do," said Arthur, matter of factly, "because the skin on them is starting to peel off!"

"Ugh!" Frank was feeling very sick. "I'm coming apart at the seams!"

"It's just the wrinkles dropping off!"

said Arthur.

The peeling started at Frank's feet and moved down his body to his head. He looked like a large pink snake, shedding its unwanted skin. The dry, crispy white flakes floated to the floor like thin pieces of rice paper, and covered the carpet.

"What's happening to me?" said Frank.

"We've reversed the ageing process!" said Arthur. He was so happy that he didn't know whether to suck his thumb or not. It went in and out of his mouth like a lollipop until, eventually, he sat on it. "We've turned back the sands of time!"

"Help!" squeaked Frank, suddenly. "My voice! I can't control it!"

"It's going back to how it was before," said Arthur. "And look at your hair!"

"How can I look at my hair, you weedy cheeseball! It's on the top of my head." Frank was turning back into the Frank of old.

"It's growing back!" cheered Arthur. "I've never seen anything sprout so fast! It's amazing!"

"Listen, Arthur," said Frank, "if you don't get me down from here, I'll bash you black and blue!"

"That's charming," said Arthur. "After all that I've done for you."

"Do you want a chinese burn, or what!" threatened Frank.

"What's the 'or what'?" asked Arthur, cautiously.

"A bunch of fives in the kisser!" said Frank, bluntly.

"Oh, dear," said Arthur. "I think you must be back to normal."

Frank was indeed back to normal. Back to eight-year-old Frank, the big, beastly, bullying elder brother.

Arthur cut him down. Frank fell on to his back, rubbed his ankles and stood up. Arthur couldn't tell whether Frank was angry or not. His eyebrows were knitted together like two amorous caterpillars, and his mouth was ever so slightly pinched. Frank took one step forward, and growled. Arthur braced himself for his first clip round the ear in weeks. Frank raised his arms and threw them round Arthur's neck.

"Thanks!" he said. "You've saved my life!"

"It was nothing," replied Arthur.

"I know," said Frank.

At that moment, they heard a noise outside their bedroom window. It was the clang of Old Ma McCracken's big, black iron gates. The brothers opened the curtains just wide enough to peek out. The stretch-limousine was still parked in the road. Two bodyguards, wearing red tartan kilts and dark glasses were helping The Dreaded Lurgie, who was dressed up like a dog's dinner, to climb into the back of it.

"She's leaving for Humptys!" whispered Arthur.

"Then we must stop her."

"Shouldn't we tell someone that we've found a cure first?"

"There isn't time," said Frank. "If she hears that we're on to her, she'll disappear. Then, we'll never find her, and if we can't find her, we won't be able to stop her from spreading the Snoggle Spots at some later date. We've got to capture her now, while she's out in the open!"

"Where are you going?" asked Arthur. Frank was heading for the bedroom door.

"Humptys," said Frank.

"But you've still got your pyjamas on!"

"So have you!" said Frank. "Come on!"

Why Frank and Arthur always had to go out in their pyjamas is beyond me. It was beyond Nora, too.

"Where are you going?" she demanded, as she came back into the bedroom.

"Out!" said Frank.

"But I've just phoned your parents," she protested. "They're on their way home now."

"Sorry, can't stop!" exclaimed Frank. "Got to save the world!"

Nora suddenly noticed that Frank was a little boy again. It was as if she had been smacked full in the face with a flat iron. "Frank?" she stammered. "Frank, what's happened to you?"

"I'll explain later," he replied. "Right now we've got to get to Humptys to stop your evil aunt."

"Why?" cried Nora. "No. You can't. You mustn't. You're not allowed to hurt her. She's an old lady. You'll kill her!"

"That's the general idea, actually," said Arthur, who had run back into the room to retrieve the phial of poison and the boiled sweet off the mantelpiece.

"But she's my aunt," shouted Nora, defiantly. "It doesn't matter what she's done, I can't let you kill her!"

Frank took one look at Arthur and Arthur nodded. They both knew exactly what had to be done. Arthur rushed headlong at Nora and butted her in the stomach with his forehead. She fell backwards on to Frank's bed. "Sorry," said Arthur, "but this is for everyone's good. Yours included." Then the two boys dashed out of the bedroom and locked the door.

Nora heard them go out through the front door. "Oh, crumbs!" she muttered nervously to herself. "Crumbs and double crumbs! This doesn't look good. The nanny held prisoner in a locked bedroom, her two charges gallivanting about London in their pyjamas and the parents on their way home. I don't think I'm going to be very popular!" She looked around the room and noticed the mess. "Perhaps if I tidy up, Mr and Mrs Fleming won't be quite so angry with me," she told herself. Then, she bent down, picked up a pile of Frank's dead skin off the floor, and stacked it neatly in the drawer with his tracksuits.

Chapter 23

Humptys

Regent Street was ablaze with brightly coloured bunting. Huge red, white and blue flags flew from every lamppost, balloons fluttered from doorways, and a neon sign, suspended across the street, proclaimed:

The traffic was terrible. Black taxi cabs filed up and down the street three abreast, like soldier ants. They deposited their passengers outside Humptys, then went off in search of new customers. There were so

253

many people in London for the Glam Gran Jamboree that new customers were not difficult to find.

Humptys itself was crammed full of people, most of them children. There was a queue outside the toy shop, which stretched as far up as Regent's Park in one direction, and as far down as Nelson's Column in the other. All the children who had missed Granny McCracken on her tour had turned up today, in the hope of catching a glimpse of the nation's most Glamorous Granny and of tasting one of her famous boiled sweets.

Floating high above the store was a hot air balloon, jam-packed with them. The highlight of the festivities was to be a *Grand Cascade*, when Granny McCracken herself would release the special trap door in the balloon's basket and flood Regent Street with her irresistible, poisoned sweeties.

The police cordon held firm, as the stretch-limousine edged its way across Piccadilly Circus and up into Regent Street. Old Ma McCracken felt like the Queen Mother as she waved to the rows and rows of smiling faces, which were pressed up against the car window. "I'm most terribly sorry," she muttered under her breath. The painted red smile did not leave her face for a second. "But you've all got to go!" She chortled into her handkerchief and told the driver to step on it. The driver did as he was told and ran over a policeman's foot.

The conductor of the brass band caught sight of the stretch-limousine through the crowds. He turned to face his musicians and tapped his baton on the lectern in front of him. "In the key of C," he growled. "A-one, a-two, a-three, four, five, six. . ." The band started to play a rousing march entitled "Suffer Little Children" which Old Ma McCracken had chosen specially for the occasion. It warmed her heart to hear it.

The dignitaries inside Humptys were getting very nervous with the imminent arrival of their celebrity. The head of the organizing committee was a wiry man with dandruff on his astrakan collar. His nails were bitten down to the quick and his tongue darted in and out of his mouth as he flicked uneasily through the programme of events. Suddenly, he lifted his eyes and stared around the entrance hall.

"I can't find the red carpet! Where's the

red carpet?" he panicked, tugging at his spotted green bow tie.

"You're standing on it," said the Lord Mayor of London.

"So I am! Silly me!" replied the head of the organizing committee. "Now, does everyone know what to do when Granny McCracken arrives?" he added tediously for the fifteenth time.

"Yes!" came the tired answer from the crowd.

"Well, what do I do, because I can't remember!" shrieked the organizer, who would have been better off organizing a local flower show.

"Just leave it to me," said the Lord Mayor, who had had enough of his high-pitched warblings. Then he trod on the organizer's toe and sent him screaming to the First Aid post to receive treatment.

"Well done," said the Prime Minister. "I thought we'd never get rid of him!"

A loud fanfare suddenly burst through the kerfuffle and announced Old Ma McCracken's arrival. She stepped out of the stretch-limousine to a deafening cheer from the crowd, that would have cracked the glass in Concorde's cabin windows had Concorde been flying overhead at that precise moment. She nodded and waved her way across the pavement, and turned to address the people before she entered the toy shop.

"Thank you," she said. "You have made an old woman very, very happy! I hope that you will allow me to repay your kindness and generosity in my own humble wee way!" Then, she took a handful of sweets from her handbag and threw them into a crowd of children. "And now," she continued, pausing only to kiss a sweet little red-haired girl with pigtails, "let the children come forward. Let the biggest and best free jamboree since jamborees began, begin!"

The doors to Humptys were flung open wide and the partying commenced. Waitresses rushed hither and thither carrying large platters piled high with sausages on sticks and jam sandwiches. Sacks full of crisps were lowered from the ceiling and slashed open at the bottom, so that the children could indulge themselves in a never ending orgy of crunch-filled delights. Orange squash flowed like water.

Chocolate biscuits were snapped up by the barrel-load. Conjurers, acrobats, elephant handlers and clowns with custard pies wandered through the toy store, pulling faces and performing magical feats of mindboggling complexity, and ten thousand people played a huge game of pass the parcel in the street.

At the centre of all this merrymaking sat old Ma McCracken, looking like Santa

Claus in his grotto. She was surrounded by hundreds of laughing children, and she had time for them all, each and every one.

"What a splendid example she is," observed the Prime Minister.

"Indeed," agreed the Lord Mayor. "Not only has she kissed every child here today, but they have all received a boiled sweet, too!"

Well, not *every* child. Not yet. But the old witch was working on it!

While all of this was going on, another crowd had formed outside Buckingham Palace. A group of startled American tourists were watching two boys pedalling furiously down The Mall in their pyjamas.

"The party will have started by now!" shouted Frank, who was struggling to make himself heard above the traffic.

"I'm puffed out!" yelled Arthur in reply. Then he added, "What do we do when we get there?"

"I have a plan," bellowed Frank.

"Is it a good one?" shrieked Arthur.

"I don't know," roared Frank, "but it's a

plan, and it's the only one we've got, so we'd better make the most of it."

Arthur whistled for Frank to stop. "Listen," he said, coming up alongside his brother, "it's all very well having a plan, in fact, I'm grateful that you've thought of one, but a plan is not much use to anyone unless it's a GOOD one!"

Frank thought hard for a moment. "It's a good one," he said.

"OK," said Arthur. "Then, let's do it!"

Nobody paid the slightest attention to Frank and Arthur as they wheeled their bicycles into Humptys and stood them up in the middle of a display of brand new bikes.

"Perfect disguise," said Frank, winking at Arthur. Arthur liked the way that Frank could wink. It was good to have something to admire in your elders.

They plunged into the middle of the crowd, which was surging, like a mighty river, towards the escalator.

"All these people will be going upstairs to see Old Ma McCracken," said Arthur.

"Exactly," replied Frank. "Stick with them and we'll find her."

"You still haven't told me what to do when we get there," Arthur said, niftily side-stepping a large boot which missed his slippered foot by inches. "There are an awful lot of people here, aren't there?" he added. It was quite scary.

"We're going to make her suck that boiled sweet that you've got in your pocket," said Frank.

"How?" asked Arthur. "We can't just go up to her and say, 'Hello, Old Ma McCracken, would you suck this deadly, poisonous sweet for us, please?' She won't do it."

"We're going to distract her," said Frank, proudly.

"How?"

"Will you stop saying, how!" barked Frank. "I don't know. We'll think of something when we get up there!"

Arthur glowered at his brother. Then, he muttered, under his breath, "It doesn't sound like a very GOOD plan, at all!"

As the escalator climbed further up the store, Frank and Arthur noticed more and more children going down in the opposite direction, with looks of perfect happiness on their faces. They were all sucking boiled sweets, and the flavour was out of this world.

"We're getting closer," whispered Frank. "Synchronize watches!"

"What does that mean?" said Arthur.

"It's what they always do in the movies before a big mission," said Frank.

"Yes, but what does it mean?"

"It means," sighed Frank, who was fed up with having to explain everything to Arthur, "that we've got to put our watches right."

"Why?" asked Arthur.

"JUST DO IT!" shouted Frank.

"OK, OK!" said Arthur, defensively. Frank was very tense.

"Have you done it?" demanded Frank.

"Er. . . No," replied his brother.

"Well, why not?"

"Because I haven't got a watch!" blubbed Arthur. He was close to tears, and Frank thought it best not to push the synchronizing of their watches any further. Besides, he didn't know why they needed to do it, either.

The Dreaded Lurgie was on the top floor. Frank and Arthur could hear her voice as they approached the end of the escalator. It cut through the general hubbub like a bat's squeak. When they saw her, she was sitting on a red velvet throne at the far end of the room. To her right was a barrel of sweets. Behind her stood the two kilted bodyguards. In front, a long line of excited children snaked its way in and out of the shelves of toys.

"Join the queue," said Frank to Arthur. "Pretend you're here to meet the nation's favourite granny. Make sure that you sit on her knee. Then, when I give the signal, just pop the sweet into her mouth."

"What if she spits it out?" asked Arthur.

"Hold her jaws together . . . like this," said Frank, demonstrating on his younger brother.

"Ow!" said Arthur, when Frank had let go. "That hurt! And what are you going to be doing?"

"I'm the diversion," said Frank, making it sound like the most dangerous job. "Don't you worry about me."

"I wasn't," admitted Arthur. "I was more worried about *me*, actually!"

Then, they split up. Frank went towards a shelf full of practical jokes, and Arthur joined the end of the queue.

The queue moved very slowly. Old Ma McCracken was making sure that every child got the correct dose of her foul poison. She was doing so much kissing and wiping and handing out of boiled sweets, that Arthur was scared she might fall asleep before his turn came round. But he needn't have worried. Old Ma McCracken was having the time of her life. She was revelling in the apogee of her evil scheme. Sleep was far from her mind.

As he got closer to The Dreaded Lurgie, Arthur felt his heartbeat quicken. His mouth dried up and his hands became sticky. He practised trying to sound normal, but his voice had taken on a life of its own. It quivered and wobbled like a record playing first at 33, and then at 78. "Calm down," he said to himself, but when he looked at the two bodyguards standing by her side, he found that calming down was completely impossible.

"Who's next?" queried Granny McCracken, smiling broadly. A strong pair of hands clasped Arthur round the waist and lifted him on to the old woman's knee. She ran her bony fingers through his blond curls.

"My, my," she said. "Haven't we met before?"

"Er. . . No," said Arthur. He hoped that she could not feel him trembling.

"Then, what's your name?"

Arthur could feel her black eyes boring through his head and peering into his brain. She was trying to find out what he was thinking!

"My name is Joseph," he lied. That would confuse her.

"Joseph who?" queried The Dreaded Lurgie.

Arthur was stumped. He searched for inspiration.

"Joseph Remote Controlled Tank," he said. That was stupid! Now she was sure to realize that he was up to something.

"Where's your brother?" Old Ma McCracken asked, suddenly.

"I don't have a brother," stammered Arthur.

"Your brother Frank!"

She was on to him! Old Ma McCracken had recognized him as the boy next door. Where *was* Frank? Where was his diversion?

The Dreaded Lurgie tightened her grip on Arthur's arms. "You are a naughty boy, Arthur. Were you hoping to come here today and ruin Granny McCracken's little surprise?"

"No," he gasped. She was squeezing the breath out of him.

"It won't work! I'm much stronger than you. I can make you do whatever I want!" She had hold of his jaw now, and was fishing around in the barrel for a boiled sweet. "If at first you don't succeed," she cackled, "suck a sweet, instead! Now, eat this up like a good little boy! Eat it all up for Granny McCracken!" The sweet was unwrapped and Arthur could not get his mouth closed.

"Frank!" he cried. "Frank!" But she had such a tight grip on his jaw, that it came out sounding like "thanks".

"It's my pleasure," snickered Old Ma McCracken, with a triumphant glint in her eye.

Suddenly, a voice boomed out from

behind the model counter.

"NOW!" it screamed. A remote controlled aeroplane swooped down from the ceiling and dive-bombed The Dreaded Lurgie. It came in low across her right shoulder, banked steeply to the left and removed her wig with its undercarriage. She threw her hands up to protect herself, and let go of Arthur.

"Over there!" she shouted, pointing Frank out to her bodyguards. She didn't see Arthur take the boiled sweet out from his pocket and unwrap it. "Catch him!" she yelled. "Bring me his head on a plate!" She was popping mad. The veins in her black eyes had exploded into a riot of red and pink fireworks. Her drooling tongue hung from the corner of her mouth, like a panting dog's.

The bodyguards leapt over the throne and flattened a line of screaming children like dominoes. Frank was ready for them. He dropped the remote control unit and kicked three footballs into their path, followed by six bags of marbles and a pair of roller skates. The bodyguards hit the lot going full tilt. They skidded and slid across the floor in a flurry of tartan. Then, with

one cataclysmic crash, they hurtled headlong into a huge pyramid of wooden building bricks. It tumbled down on top of them and buried them alive.

"Now, Arthur!" screamed Frank for the second time, rushing forward and pouring several large packets of itching powder down the bodyguards' backs. "Do it now!"

Arthur had been spellbound by the speed of events and had forgotten to put the boiled sweet into Old Ma McCracken's mouth. He had given her the time she had needed to guess what they were up to. She flung Arthur to the floor and made a dash for the escalators.

"What's going on?" said the Lord Mayor.

"A game of Tag, I think," said the Prime Minister. "Isn't she wonderful for her age!"

Arthur picked himself up. He was bruised, but not beaten. "She's getting away!" he shouted.

"Quick! Chuck me the sweet," said Frank, picking up a baseball bat. "And make sure you throw it up high!" Arthur did as he was told. He lobbed the sweet high into the air towards his brother. Frank met it with a perfect drive. The boiled sweet flipped back across the room and sped straight towards the powdered nose of the United Kingdom's most Glamorous Granny.

"You won't get away with this," she screamed, turning to face Frank at the top of the escalator. "I'll crunch you, I'll scrunch you, I'll mash you up and munch you!"

She should never have turned around. Nor, indeed, should she ever have opened her great big mouth, because that was her undoing.

The boiled sweet, hit so accurately by Frank, plunged straight down the back of The Dreaded Lurgie's throat!

The room fell silent, as Old Ma McCracken staggered backwards and clutched her neck.

"What have you done?" she rasped.

"Given you a taste of your own medicine," said Arthur bravely. "Let's see how *you* like your boiled sweets!" The old woman croaked a little, then whinnied like a horse. Her eyes flashed around the room pleading for help, but none was forthcoming. People were too scared at what was happening to her. She lurched forward as the poison started to work, and crashed into a shelf of laughing false teeth. They hit the floor laughing, and laughed on, until every last bit of The Dreaded Lurgie had been destroyed.

She smoked and she bubbled. She drooped and she dribbled. She withered and crumbled away. Her skin cracked like old parchment. Her wispy grey hair turned to straw. Her fingernails grew to a thousand times their normal length. Her bones disintegrated in a swirling cloud of black dust. In the time it takes for a furnace to consume a coffin, The Dreaded Lurgie was reduced to a pile of smoking ashes. All that remained was a single black ankle boot, which slowly melted into a steaming puddle of sticky tar. Nothing that a quick flick with a damp mop and a vacuum cleaner would not clear up.

"What was that all about?" said the Prime Minister.

"She died of old age," said Arthur.

"She died of the Dreaded Lurgie," said Frank. "She was spreading the disease through those boiled sweets."

"Is that so?" said the Lord Mayor, doubtfully.

"Of course it isn't," mocked the Prime Minister. "The Dreaded Lurgie doesn't exist. Granny McCracken said so herself."

"If you think that," said Frank, "then you're as stupid as she was."

"He's had it, so he should know," piped up Arthur.

"And, for your information," said Frank, "Arthur and I are the only two people in the world who know how to cure the Dreaded Lurgie!"

"So, stick that in your pipe and smoke it!" added Arthur, defiantly.

There are things you can say to a Prime Minister, and there are things which you cannot. "Stick that in your pipe and smoke it" is one of the things you cannot say.

Arthur learnt this lesson rather quickly.

CHAPTER 24

Upside-Down Day

Mr and Mrs Fleming returned from Barbados to find their two children in prison and Nora going quietly round the twist in the bedroom. She begged their forgiveness, which they magnanimously dispensed, then packed her bags, hitched a lift to Cape Wrath and spent the rest of her days in a nunnery. Frank and Arthur had been arrested for "doing in" the United Kingdom's most Glamorous Granny. They protested their innocence and explained that Old Ma McCracken was really a witch. She hadn't liked children at all. In fact, she had loathed and detested them. That was why she had spread the Dreaded Lurgie through the boiled sweets — to make children die from old age, long before their time.

"Tosh!" said the police chief.

"Pish!" said the Lord Mayor, and . . .

"How interesting," said the Prime Minister, which took everyone by surprise. He had just come from an emergency meeting with the Queen. She had been complaining of feeling older than usual. He had asked her when this feeling had started, and she had replied, "Just after Granny McCracken came to tea and gave one one of her delicious boiled sweets." Maybe, thought the Prime Minister, there was something in what Frank and Arthur had to say, after all. Maybe, he had been wrong to ignore the protestations of his Minister for Health.

Ever quick to seize an opportunity to swim with the tide of popular opinion, the Prime Minister sent one of the boiled sweets to a top laboratory in Shropshire, with strict instructions to find out exactly what was in it. The results were astonishing. The scientists unearthed no less than seventeen age-effecting drugs. Their report concluded,

> " This sweet is a biological time bomb.
> **DO NOT LET IT FALL INTO THE WRONG HANDS!** "

"I tried to tell you, but you wouldn't listen," said the Minister for Health, as forcefully as he dared.

"Thank you," said the Prime Minister. "Now, go away. You're fired!" The Minister for Health was too weak to argue and left the Cabinet Room through the window. The Prime Minister remained unconcerned by his dramatic departure and turned round to face Frank and Arthur. "You say that you have found a cure for this Dreaded Lurgie?" he said.

"It worked for me," said Frank.

"But would it work for the whole country?" asked the Prime Minister wisely. That was why he was Prime Minister, because he knew how to ask all the right questions.

"Yes," said Arthur, "but we'd need the Queen's help to tell people what to do."

The Prime Minister laughed. "On

matters of National Importance," he crowed, "nobody sees the Queen except me."

"Then we shall just have to tell the world how you treated your Minister for Health when he was right all along," threatened Frank.

"I'll see what I can do," stammered the P.M., backpedalling faster than a circus acrobat.

And so, they were sent to visit the Queen in Buckingham Palace. They were surprised to find that someone so majestic could be quite such a yawner, but a cheek-splitting yawner she was.

"One is most dreadfully sorry," she slurred, showing Frank and Arthur the fillings in her back teeth, "but one can't seem to keep one's eyes open."

"Do you think you're getting older, your Majesty?" asked Arthur.

"Well, yes. One supposes that one is."

"I thought you probably were," said Frank, "because you look really ancient today. Much older than you look on the stamps." He smiled half-heartedly, realizing, too late, that one should never discuss such personal matters with a queen.

Arthur wanted to get to the point. "It is because you have caught the Dreaded Lurgie," he declared.

"Has one indeed?" replied the Queen.

"And I can cure you," pronounced Arthur.

"How?" she enquired.

"You've got to stand on your head."

"I beg your pardon?"

"You've got to stand on your head!"

The Queen giggled. "Queens do not stand on their heads," she said.

"Why ever not?" asked Arthur.

"Because we would look stupid, and a queen must never look stupid. She must look dignified at all times."

"Oh," said Arthur. "I hadn't thought of that."

Frank was rolling around on the Persian carpet with a corgi. Suddenly, he stopped and announced, "I've got a brilliant idea!"

The Queen seemed pleased. "Good for you," she said. "Let's hear it."

"Why not have a National Upside-Down Day," said Frank, "when everyone has to spend the day the wrong way up? Then,

your Majesty, if *everyone* is standing on their head, you *won't* look stupid!"

"A National Upside-Down Day?" mused the Queen.

"And if you tell everyone that they've got to do it, then they will, because you're the Queen. And if they don't, you chop their heads off!"

"That seems simple enough," she said.

"It does, doesn't it?" said Frank, who was rather pleased with himself.

"Oh, and one other thing," interrupted

Arthur. "Your Prime Minister."

"What about him?"

"He's not very nice, is he?"

"Not really," replied the Queen, "but there's not much one can do about it."

"Unless you turn everything upside-down on National Upside-Down Day," suggested Arthur. "Give the Parliamentary janitor the job of Prime Minister for twenty-four hours and make the Prime Minister clean out the House of Commons' loo."

"Brilliant," chuckled the Queen. "What wicked fun!"

Two days later, the Queen announced a new holiday. National Upside-Down Day was introduced into the annual calendar. It proved to be very popular as well, with everyone that is except the Prime Minister, who got blisters on his hands from wielding his mop. Not only did people seem to enjoy spending the day on their heads, and eating the Royal baker's specially prepared Upside-Down cake but, miraculously, all trace of the Dreaded Lurgie disappeared.

Great Britain, once again, sang to the sound of children's voices.

Frank and Arthur were given a medal by the Queen for services to medical science, and a bust of the two brothers can be seen to this day in the entrance hall of The British Medical Association. Arthur's, of course, is standing on its head.

Oh, and if you're wondering when National Upside-Down Day is . . . It's today.